OFFICIAL KEYART FOR CARSON KELLY PUBLISHING'S AND
CARSON KELLY'S TALKING DOGS: KELVIN'S WISH

TALKING DOGS

KELVIN'S WISH

CARSON J KELLY

CARSON KELLY PUBLISHING, LLC

ISBN-13: 9798223177111
ISBN-10: 9798223177111

Cover design by: Carson Kelly Publishing, LLC
Library of Congress Control Number: 2018675309
Printed in the United States of America

Michael Lewett Kelly

CONTENTS

INTRODUCTION: THE WORLD OF KELVIN

In a corner of the cosmos, swirling with nebulas and starlight, lies the planet BIORUTA. A jewel of nature and technology, it is home to lush forests, sprawling cities, and a unique marvel: talking dogs. These sentient canines live in harmony with humans and other beings, sharing a world where the wonders of nature and advancements of technology intertwine seamlessly.

In this world, nestled in a quaint town edged by the glow of a futuristic metropolis, lived Kelvin, a Golden Retriever with a fur as warm as his heart. His days were simple and joyful – filled with games in the garden, naps under the sun, and evenings spent with his beloved family. Little did Kelvin know, his life was about to take a turn into the realms of the extraordinary.

PROLOGUE: THE NIGHT EVERYTHING CHANGED

One tranquil night, under a tapestry of stars, something unusual stirred in Kelvin's home. The house, usually filled with the comforting sounds of family life, was gripped by a hushed urgency. Bags were packed in whispers, decisions made in silent nods. Kelvin, curled up in his bed, was oblivious to the quiet commotion.

As the clock chimed a haunting midnight melody, Kelvin's family took a lingering look at their sleeping pet. With heavy hearts, they left behind a note – simple words etched with deep meanings unknown. The door closed with a soft click, leaving Kelvin behind, the silence of the night enveloping the house once more.

When the morning sun peeked through the curtains, casting its gentle light on the note by Kelvin's bed, the stage was set for an adventure beyond the ordinary, into a world brimming with mysteries and wonders.

CHAPTER 1: THE JOURNEY BEGINS

The sun rose high over BIORUTA, its rays filtering through Kelvin's window, nudging him awake. The house was silent, unusually so. Kelvin's ears perked up; something was amiss. The familiar hustle of the morning was replaced by an echoing stillness.

Room by room, Kelvin searched for his family, his heart growing heavier with each empty space. The note left behind offered no comfort, only questions. "Gone to attend urgent matter. Back soon. Love you." The words spun in his head, a riddle without an answer.

As the day unfolded, Kelvin's concern turned into resolve. He couldn't just wait; he had to find them. He remembered tales of the city's marvels and dangers, stories of towering buildings, neon lights, and beings from across the stars. It was time to explore beyond his garden's fence.

Venturing into the city, Kelvin found himself in a world vastly different from his quiet neighborhood. Hover cars zoomed past in the sky, buildings stretched high, touching the clouds, and screens flashed with information and advertisements. The city was a symphony of sights and sounds, a maze of possibilities.

Kelvin navigated this new world with a mix of awe and determination. He encountered various beings – some helpful, others indifferent. He learned to navigate the busy streets, find food, and seek information. Each step took him deeper into the heart of BIORUTA, and closer to unraveling the mystery of his family's disappearance.

The day turned into night, and the city lights danced in Kelvin's eyes. He found a quiet spot in a park, beneath a tree that reminded him of home. As he lay there, looking up at the stars, Kelvin knew his journey had only just begun. His quest to find his family would take him to corners of BIORUTA he never knew existed, through challenges he never imagined.

In the heart of the sleeping city, a talking dog's adventure was unfolding, a journey of courage, curiosity, and the unbreakable bonds of family.

The night in the city brought a different kind of beauty, with neon lights painting the sky in a kaleidoscope of colors. Kelvin, though tired, felt a sense of excitement. The city was vast, and his family could be anywhere, but he was determined to find them.

As he wandered through the bustling streets, Kelvin realized he needed a plan. He decided to start by visiting places his family loved, hoping to find a clue or a familiar face. His journey took him to the city's central park, a place of greenery amidst the concrete, where he and his family had spent many happy afternoons.

The park, under the moon's soft glow, was peaceful. Kelvin sniffed around, his senses heightened, searching for any trace of his family. He roamed past the familiar pond, the playground, and the winding paths lined with flowers. But as the night deepened, so did his realization that this path might not lead him to them.

Not one to give up, Kelvin decided to explore other parts of the city. His travels led him through bustling marketplaces filled with exotic goods, quiet residential areas with gardens mirroring his own, and to the outskirts of the city, where the urban landscape met the wild beauty of nature.

Along the way, Kelvin met various characters – a friendly robotic street cleaner who offered him water, a group of stray animals who shared their tales of city life, and a wise old owl who spoke of the changes in BIORUTA. Each encounter provided Kelvin with a piece of the city's puzzle, but not the one he was desperately looking for.

As dawn broke, painting the sky in hues of pink and orange, Kelvin found himself at a small café he had often visited with his family. The owner, recognizing Kelvin, greeted him with surprise and concern. "Kelvin, what are you doing here all alone?" she asked.

Kelvin explained his situation, and the café owner, Mrs. Rivera, listened sympathetically. "I haven't seen your family, Kelvin, but I'll keep an eye out. You're welcome to stay here for a while."

Grateful for the offer, Kelvin rested at the café, gathering his strength and thoughts. He realized that his quest might be longer and more challenging than he had anticipated. But the kindness he had encountered along the way strengthened his resolve. He wasn't just a lost dog; he was a part of a community, a being on a mission fueled by love and hope.

As the café came to life with the morning rush, Kelvin set out once again, his spirit undeterred. He knew that his family was out there somewhere, and he wouldn't stop until he found them. The city, with all its mysteries and wonders, was just the beginning of his journey.

Kelvin's journey through the city continued, each day bringing new experiences and encounters. He ventured into neighborhoods he'd never seen before, each with its own unique character and inhabitants. From the high-rise apartments that touched the clouds to the quaint suburban areas reminiscent of his home, each place offered new clues and possibilities.

One day, while exploring a bustling marketplace in the heart of the city, Kelvin overheard a conversation about a gathering of talking dogs in a distant part of BIORUTA. His ears perked up at the mention. Perhaps, he thought, someone there might know something about his family.

Determined to follow this new lead, Kelvin set out on his longest journey yet. He traveled through varied landscapes – past rolling hills, across wide rivers, and through dense forests. Each step took him further from the city but closer to a potential reunion with his family.

Along the way, Kelvin encountered other animals and beings, each with their own stories and insights. He met a group of traveling musicians, a band of friendly nomads, and a wise old turtle who spoke of the ancient history of BIORUTA. From each, Kelvin learned more about the world he lived in – its beauty, its diversity, and its complexities.

Finally, after several days of travel, Kelvin arrived at the gathering of talking dogs. It was a vibrant assembly, with dogs of all breeds and sizes coming together to share stories, play, and learn from one another. Kelvin was welcomed with open paws, his story striking a chord with many.

He eagerly asked around about his family, describing them in detail to anyone who would listen. While no one had seen them, many offered help and advice. Kelvin's story spread through the gathering, and soon, many were talking about the brave Golden Retriever on a quest to find his family.

During his time at the gathering, Kelvin learned important skills that would help him on his journey. He learned how to read the stars for direction, how to find food and water in the wilderness, and how to communicate more effectively with different species. He left the gathering not just with new knowledge, but also with a network of friends and allies who promised to keep an eye out for his family.

With renewed hope and determination, Kelvin set off once again. He now knew that his journey was not just about finding his family, but also about discovering the rich tapestry of life and connections that made up BIORUTA. Each encounter, each challenge, was shaping him into a wiser, stronger individual.

As he left the gathering behind, heading towards the unknown, Kelvin realized that no matter how far he traveled, he carried with him the love of his family and the support of new friends. His adventure was more than a search; it was a journey of growth, discovery, and the unbreakable bonds of love and friendship.

Kelvin's journey through BIORUTA continued with a newfound sense of purpose. Each day brought its own set of challenges and wonders, and each night, under the starlit sky, he reflected on the lessons learned and the friendships forged.

His travels took him through the sprawling meadows of the Great Plains, where the grass danced in the wind and the horizon stretched endlessly. Here, Kelvin encountered a herd of talking horses, majestic creatures who spoke of the history of the plains and the ancient spirits that roamed them. They shared tales of a hidden valley, a place of serenity and magic, which piqued Kelvin's interest. Could his family have passed through there?

Eager to explore every possibility, Kelvin journeyed to the hidden valley. The path was not easy; it wound through rugged terrain and dense forests. But the beauty of the valley, when he finally arrived, took his breath away. It was a tranquil paradise, untouched by time, with crystal-clear streams and flowers that glowed in the moonlight.

In the heart of the valley, Kelvin found a small, peaceful community of various creatures living in harmony. They welcomed him with kindness, offering shelter and food. Kelvin inquired about his family, describing them to every inhabitant he met. While no one had seen them, they all listened to his story with empathy and offered words of encouragement.

One evening, while sharing stories around a fire, an elderly owl perched on a nearby tree spoke up. "Your quest is noble, young one," the owl said in a wise, deep voice. "The bonds of family and love are strong. You must look not only with your eyes but also with your heart. Sometimes what we seek is not just a place or a person, but a feeling, a connection."

These words resonated with Kelvin. He realized that his journey was more than a physical search; it was a spiritual journey, connecting him with the heart of BIORUTA and its inhabitants.

Inspired by the owl's wisdom, Kelvin decided to visit the Mystic Peaks, a mountain range said to be the dwelling of ancient spirits and keepers of the planet's deepest secrets. The journey to the peaks was arduous, taking him through steep trails and across treacherous passes. But Kelvin's determination did not waver.

At the summit, Kelvin found himself above the clouds, the world below a tapestry of colors and forms. Here, he met a wise old eagle, known as the Guardian of the Peaks. The eagle had watched over BIORUTA for centuries, and its eyes held the depth of the universe.

Kelvin shared his story with the Guardian, who listened intently, its gaze piercing through to Kelvin's soul. "Your family's path is intertwined with the destiny of BIORUTA," the eagle spoke in a voice that echoed like the wind. "Your journey is part of a larger tapestry, woven with threads of love, courage, and destiny. Keep your heart open, and you will find the answers you seek."

Filled with a sense of awe and a deeper understanding of his quest, Kelvin descended from the Mystic Peaks, his heart lighter and his resolve stronger. He knew that his journey was about more than finding his family; it was about understanding the interconnectedness of all life on BIORUTA and the cosmic forces that bound them.

Kelvin's adventure takes him through the wonders of BIORUTA, each step bringing new insights and deepening his connection to the planet and its inhabitants. His quest has become a journey of discovery, not just of his family but of the mysteries and magic of the world around him.

Kelvin, with the Guardian of the Peaks' words echoing in his mind, ventured onward, his spirit filled with a newfound wisdom. His path now took him to the Coastal Realms, where the land met the vast, uncharted oceans of BIORUTA. The shores were lined with cliffs and sandy beaches, and the air was filled with the salty scent of the sea.

In a small coastal village, Kelvin encountered a group of sea creatures who spoke of the wonders beneath the waves – of underwater cities and coral forests glowing in the depths. Intrigued by these tales, Kelvin wondered if his family's journey had taken them to these mysterious underwater realms.

While exploring the coastline, Kelvin came across a pod of talking dolphins playing in the waves. They were joyful and friendly, and upon hearing Kelvin's story, offered to take him on a tour of the coastal waters. Kelvin, thrilled at the opportunity, joined them, marveling at the beauty of the ocean and the life it harbored.

The dolphins showed Kelvin coral reefs teeming with colorful fish, underwater caves with walls covered in bioluminescent algae, and deep-sea trenches where ancient creatures lurked. The ocean was a world of its own, vast and full of mysteries.

After his underwater adventure, Kelvin thanked the dolphins and returned to the shore. The visit to the ocean had opened his eyes to the diversity of life on BIORUTA, each part of the planet offering unique experiences and inhabitants.

Continuing his journey, Kelvin ventured into the Duskwood Forest, a place of enchantment and mystery. The forest was said to be home to mystical beings and ancient magic. As he walked under the towering trees, the light dimmed, and the forest floor was illuminated by the soft glow of fireflies.

In the heart of Duskwood, Kelvin came upon a clearing where a serene pond lay. The water was clear and still, reflecting the stars and the moon in its surface. It was said that the pond had reflective powers, showing not just images but also visions and truths.

Kelvin peered into the pond, and to his surprise, he saw not his own reflection, but glimpses of his family's journey – images of them traveling through various landscapes, meeting different beings, and overcoming challenges. The visions were fragmented, like pieces of a puzzle, but they reinforced Kelvin's belief that he was on the right path.

The time in Duskwood Forest passed peacefully, and Kelvin left the mystical woods feeling rejuvenated and hopeful. His journey had taken him across BIORUTA, through cities, oceans, and forests, each step revealing more about the planet and its secrets.

Kelvin's adventure was more than a search for his family; it was a journey of self-discovery and a testament to the enduring power of love and determination. As he continued on his path, Kelvin knew that each experience was shaping him, preparing him for the reunion with his family and the role he was to play in the greater story of BIORUTA.

Kelvin's journey next led him to the Whispering Highlands, a region of rolling hills and quiet valleys, where the wind carried voices from the past. The highlands were known for their ancient ruins and stone circles, remnants of a time long gone but not forgotten.

As he trekked through the highlands, Kelvin felt a sense of serenity. The wind whispered stories in his ears, tales of the ancient inhabitants of BIORUTA, their wisdom, and their connection to the land. Among the ruins, Kelvin found carvings and symbols that spoke of the harmony between the planet and the stars, echoing the lessons he had learned from the Guardians and the elders.

One evening, while resting near a stone circle, Kelvin was approached by a flock of luminescent birds. These birds were the keepers of stories, collecting tales from across BIORUTA and sharing them with those who would listen. They sang to Kelvin, their melodies weaving stories of adventures and heroes, of love and loss. Each song was a thread in the tapestry of BIORUTA's history, and Kelvin listened with a heart full of wonder.

The stories of the luminescent birds inspired Kelvin. He realized that his own journey was becoming a part of BIORUTA's rich history. His quest to find his family had turned into a journey of discovery, uncovering the secrets of the planet and understanding the interconnectedness of all its inhabitants.

Leaving the Whispering Highlands, Kelvin journeyed to the city of Solaris, a place where technology and magic blended seamlessly. Solaris was a hub of innovation and knowledge, its libraries and academies a treasure trove of information.

In Solaris, Kelvin sought knowledge about the celestial events and the cosmic energies that the guardians had spoken of. He delved into ancient texts and spoke with scholars and mages, each providing pieces to the puzzle of his family's journey. He learned about the alignments of planets and stars, about gateways to other dimensions, and about the ancient protectors of BIORUTA.

With each new piece of knowledge, Kelvin felt closer to finding his family. He understood that their disappearance was linked to something much larger than he had initially thought. They were part of a cosmic cycle, guardians of a legacy that spanned millennia.

Armed with this new understanding, Kelvin knew that his journey was far from over. There were still places to explore, secrets to uncover, and connections to be made. The city of Solaris was just another step in his journey, a journey that was shaping him into a guardian in his own right.

Kelvin left Solaris with a sense of purpose. He had come far from the dog who had set out from his home, filled with worry and uncertainty. Now, he was a traveler, a seeker of truths, and a part of the great story of BIORUTA. His heart was full of hope, and his spirit was ready for the adventures that awaited him. The journey to find his family had become a journey of becoming, of stepping into a role that was waiting for him since the stars first shone over BIORUTA.

Kelvin's next destination was the Caverns of Echoes, a mystical network of underground tunnels known for their ability to carry sounds over great distances. Legends spoke of these caverns as places where one could hear the echoes of the past and whispers of the future.

As he navigated the intricate pathways of the caverns, Kelvin's paws echoed on the ancient stone. The walls were lined with luminous crystals that cast a soft, otherworldly glow. In the depths of the caverns, he found pools of crystal-clear water that reflected the light, creating a tapestry of shimmering colors.

In these echoing halls, Kelvin felt a profound connection to the planet. The whispers of the caverns spoke to him, not in words, but in feelings and visions. He saw fleeting glimpses of his family, their faces illuminated by the same crystal light that surrounded him. These visions, though brief, filled Kelvin with a sense of urgency and hope. His family was out there, somewhere, and he was drawing closer to them with each step.

Emerging from the Caverns of Echoes, Kelvin found himself in the Valley of Mists, a place shrouded in perpetual fog and mystery. The valley was said to be home to ancient spirits and rare creatures, a place where the veil between worlds was thin.

As he journeyed through the mist, Kelvin encountered beings of light and shadow, each with their own story to tell. Some offered guidance, while others posed riddles and challenges. Kelvin's journey through the valley was a test of his resolve and his ability to trust his instincts.

One particularly mystical encounter in the valley was with an age-old spirit known as the Weaver of Fates. This ethereal entity wove the threads of destiny, and it spoke to Kelvin of the intricate web of life and the importance of each being's role in the tapestry of the universe.

"You are more than a seeker, Kelvin," the Weaver of Fates whispered in a voice like the rustling of leaves. "Your journey is a thread in the fabric of the cosmos, intertwined with the destinies of many."

Inspired by this encounter, Kelvin continued his journey with a renewed sense of purpose. He understood that his quest to find his family was part of a larger narrative, one that encompassed the past, present, and future of BIORUTA.

As the Valley of Mists gave way to the open skies, Kelvin found himself on the edge of the Great Expanse, a vast wilderness that stretched to the horizons. Here, the land was wild and untamed, full of natural wonders and hidden dangers.

Kelvin traversed the Great Expanse, encountering its diverse inhabitants and learning from them. He met wandering hermits who shared ancient lore, playful sprites that danced in the moonlight, and wise beasts that spoke of the balance of nature.

Each encounter, each challenge, and each revelation on his journey added to Kelvin's understanding of BIORUTA and his place in it. He was no longer just searching for his family; he was learning about the interconnectedness of all life and the delicate balance that sustained it.

The end of this leg of his journey brought Kelvin to the edge of the Twilight Sea, a vast body of water that sparkled under the setting sun. As he gazed out over the horizon, where the sea met the sky, Kelvin knew that his adventure was far from over. There were still many paths to explore, mysteries to unravel, and truths to uncover.

With the vast expanse of BIORUTA stretching out before him, Kelvin stepped forward, ready to continue his journey. His heart was filled with the love of his family, the wisdom of the planet, and the courage to face whatever lay ahead. His adventure was a testament to the power of hope, the strength of spirit, and the unending quest for understanding in the wondrous world of BIORUTA.

Standing at the shores of the Twilight Sea, Kelvin reflected on his journey thus far. The sea, with its endless expanse and rhythmic waves, seemed to echo the vastness of his quest. But rather than feeling daunted, Kelvin felt invigorated. The sea was a reminder of the endless possibilities that lay before him.

Determined to leave no stone unturned, Kelvin decided to venture along the coastline. The beach was a blend of rugged cliffs and soft sands, with the sea breeze carrying the scent of salt and adventure. As he traveled, he came across fishermen and sea travelers, each with their own stories of the ocean's wonders and perils.

One particular tale caught Kelvin's attention – a story of an island that appeared only during certain phases of the moon, a place said to be a bridge between the physical world and the realms of ancient magic. Intrigued by the possibility that his family might have sought out such a place, Kelvin waited for the night of the next full moon.

As the moon cast its silvery glow over the sea, an island slowly emerged from the mist, just as the fishermen had described. Kelvin, filled with a mix of excitement and apprehension, found a way to the island with the help of a kind boatman who was intrigued by the talking dog and his remarkable quest.

The island was an enchanting place, shrouded in an aura of mystery. Ancient trees whispered secrets with their rustling leaves, and streams flowed with water that sparkled under the moonlight. Kelvin explored the island, his senses alert to any sign of his family or clues to their journey.

In the heart of the island, Kelvin discovered an ancient altar, surrounded by statues that seemed to watch over it. The altar was adorned with symbols and gemstones that glowed softly in the moonlight. As he approached, the air around him tingled with a latent energy, a connection to something ancient and profound.

Kelvin couldn't help but feel that this place was significant, a piece in the puzzle of his family's disappearance. He spent the night on the island, under the watchful gaze of the moon and stars, pondering his next steps.

As dawn broke, the island began to fade, slowly being reclaimed by the sea and mist. Kelvin returned to the mainland, his mind swirling with thoughts and theories about what he had witnessed.

Continuing his journey along the coast, Kelvin encountered various coastal villages and towns, each with their own customs and stories. He shared tales of his journey, gaining not only information but also a reputation as a brave and determined explorer.

His travels eventually led him to a city known for its scholars and libraries. Here, Kelvin hoped to find more information about the celestial events and ancient magic he had encountered. The city was a trove of knowledge, with vast collections of books and scrolls.

Kelvin spent days poring over texts and speaking with scholars, piecing together the history of BIORUTA and its connection to the cosmos. He learned about the cycles of the stars, the flows of magical energies, and the legends of the guardians who had once protected the planet.

Armed with this new knowledge, Kelvin knew that his journey was far from over. The more he learned, the more he realized how much there was still to discover. His family's disappearance was a small thread in a much larger tapestry, one that spanned the history and future of BIORUTA.

With a heart full of determination and a spirit of adventure, Kelvin set out from the city, ready to follow wherever the next clue might lead. His journey was a testament to the enduring bonds of family, the quest for knowledge, and the unbreakable spirit of exploration. In the vast and wondrous world of BIORUTA, Kelvin's adventure continued, each step a part of a larger journey, each discovery a piece of an ever-unfolding mystery.

Kelvin's journey led him next to the Fabled Forests of Yarim, a mystical region known for its ancient trees that were said to have stood for thousands of years. The forest was a place of deep magic and lore, a haven for creatures both common and rare, and a repository of the planet's oldest secrets.

As he wandered through the towering trees, Kelvin felt a deep sense of reverence. The forest seemed to breathe with a life of its own, each tree whispering stories of the past. The air was thick with the scent of moss and earth, and the light that filtered through the canopy cast a greenish hue, bathing everything in an ethereal glow.

In the heart of the forest, Kelvin came across a clearing where a grand tree stood, its branches reaching high into the sky, and its roots delving deep into the earth. This tree was known as the Tree of Whispering Leaves, an ancient being that was said to hold the memories of the forest.

Approaching the tree, Kelvin felt a strange sensation, as if he were being watched. He introduced himself, and to his surprise, the tree responded. Its voice was like the rustling of leaves, ancient and wise. The Tree of Whispering Leaves spoke of the cycles of life and the deep connections that bound all beings of BIORUTA.

Kelvin shared his story with the tree, speaking of his quest to find his family and the adventures he had encountered along the way. The tree listened intently, its leaves rustling softly. After a moment of silence, the tree imparted to Kelvin a piece of advice, "Look not only where the sun shines, but also where the shadows fall. In the balance of light and dark, you will find what you seek."

Thanking the Tree of Whispering Leaves for its wisdom, Kelvin continued his exploration of the forest. He encountered various creatures, each with their own tales and insights. Some spoke of a hidden valley where time flowed differently, others of a lake that mirrored the stars, revealing the secrets of the night sky.

Each story, each encounter added to Kelvin's understanding of the world and the mysteries he was unraveling. The forest was not just a place of magic and lore; it was a living library, a keeper of knowledge and history.

As he left the Fabled Forests of Yarim, Kelvin felt a deep sense of connection with BIORUTA and its many wonders. His journey had taken him across diverse landscapes, each with its own beauty and secrets. The quest to find his family had become a journey of discovery, revealing the interconnectedness of all life and the delicate balance that sustained the planet.

With each step, Kelvin's resolve grew stronger. He was determined to find his family and uncover the truth behind their disappearance. The journey ahead was still long, and the mysteries of BIORUTA were deep and complex. But Kelvin was ready to face whatever challenges lay ahead, armed with the knowledge and wisdom he had gained.

In the vast and wondrous world of BIORUTA, Kelvin's adventure continued, a journey of courage, hope, and the unbreakable bonds of family. Each discovery was a step closer to finding his family, and each experience a part of the great tapestry of life that wove together the story of Kelvin and the planet he called home.

Kelvin's journey next led him to the Skyward Peaks, a majestic mountain range that was said to touch the heavens. The peaks were known for their mystical properties, often shrouded in clouds and glowing with an otherworldly light. It was believed that these mountains held the key to many of BIORUTA's oldest mysteries.

As Kelvin ascended the winding paths, the air grew thinner, and the scenery transformed into a breathtaking landscape of snow-capped peaks and crystal-clear skies. The view from the mountains was spectacular, offering a panorama of the diverse terrains he had traversed.

In the higher altitudes of the Skyward Peaks, Kelvin encountered a community of winged beings, graceful creatures who could soar through the skies with ease. They were guardians of the peaks, wise and ancient. They spoke to Kelvin of the stars and the celestial dance that governed the rhythms of BIORUTA.

One elder, in particular, a majestic bird with shimmering feathers, listened intently to Kelvin's tale. "Your journey is intertwined with the fabric of the universe," the elder said, its voice echoing like the wind. "The answers you seek are not just on the land but also in the alignment of the stars."

The elder showed Kelvin the ancient observatory perched atop the highest peak, where the guardians studied the stars and their secrets. Here, Kelvin learned about the cosmic events that influenced BIORUTA and the potential connections to his family's disappearance.

Armed with new knowledge and a broader perspective, Kelvin continued his ascent. At the summit, he found a place of tranquility and power, where the sky felt close enough to touch. It was here, under the canopy of the cosmos, that Kelvin felt a profound connection to his family and the journey they had undertaken.

As he gazed at the stars, Kelvin realized that his quest was about more than finding his family. It was a journey of understanding the deeper connections that bound the universe together. His family's disappearance was a piece of a larger puzzle, one that spanned the cosmos and the flow of time.

Filled with awe and determination, Kelvin descended from the Skyward Peaks, his heart and mind open to the vast mysteries of the universe. His journey across BIORUTA had taken him through enchanted forests, mystical caverns, ancient ruins, and now the soaring heights of the mountains. Each step had revealed new wonders and deepened his understanding of the world.

Kelvin knew that his adventure was far from over. There were still many paths to explore, secrets to uncover, and truths to discover. With each new day, he grew stronger, more knowledgeable, and more connected to the planet he called home.

As he set out from the Skyward Peaks, Kelvin's spirit was undaunted. He was ready for whatever lay ahead, guided by the stars and the wisdom of the many beings he had encountered. His journey was a testament to the enduring power of hope, the strength of spirit, and the quest for understanding in the magnificent world of BIORUTA.

From the lofty heights of the Skyward Peaks, Kelvin ventured into the realm known as the Shifting Sands – a vast desert that was ever-changing, its dunes reshaped by the whims of the wind. The desert was a place of both beauty and peril, its endless sands hiding secrets and challenges.

As Kelvin journeyed across the Shifting Sands, he encountered travelers and nomads, each with tales of the desert's mysteries. They spoke of mirages that showed visions, of hidden oases that appeared like apparitions, and of ancient ruins buried beneath the sands, waiting to be discovered.

One such tale that captivated Kelvin was the legend of the Mirage City, a place that appeared only under the light of the full moon. Intrigued by the possibility that his family might have sought out such a mystical location, Kelvin timed his journey to coincide with the next full moon.

Under the silver glow of the moon, Kelvin watched in awe as the Mirage City materialized before his eyes. It was a breathtaking sight – buildings and towers of sand and light, shimmering like a dream. Venturing into the city, Kelvin found it to be ethereal and silent, as if it existed in a realm between reality and illusion.

Exploring the Mirage City, Kelvin discovered carvings and artifacts that spoke of the desert's ancient history and its people's connection to the stars. It seemed that every part of BIORUTA was touched by cosmic forces, each region reflecting a different aspect of the planet's deep connection to the universe.

As the dawn approached, the Mirage City began to fade, dissolving back into the desert sands. Kelvin left the city with a sense of wonder and a deeper understanding of the desert's magic.

Continuing his travels, Kelvin encountered more of the desert's inhabitants – creatures adapted to the harsh environment, each with their own survival stories. He learned from them the ways of the desert, the secrets to finding water, and the art of navigating by the stars.

After leaving the desert, Kelvin found himself at the edge of the Crystal Forest, a mystical place where every tree and plant was made of living crystal. The forest was a spectacle of light and color, with the crystals reflecting and refracting the sunlight into rainbows.

In the Crystal Forest, Kelvin felt as if he had stepped into another world. The air was alive with energy, and the harmony between the natural world and the crystalline forms was a testament to BIORUTA's unique beauty and diversity.

Here, Kelvin encountered beings of light and energy, ethereal creatures who spoke of the balance of nature and the importance of preserving the planet's harmony. They shared with Kelvin the lore of the crystals, how they were formed by the planet's life force, and how they held the memories of the world.

Each step of Kelvin's journey through BIORUTA added to his tapestry of experiences. From the Skyward Peaks to the Shifting Sands, from the Mirage City to the Crystal Forest, Kelvin's quest had evolved into a journey of discovery, not just of his family but of the planet itself and its connection to the cosmos.

As he left the Crystal Forest, the path ahead was still unclear, but Kelvin's resolve was stronger than ever. His journey was more than a search; it was a quest for understanding, a journey into the heart of BIORUTA and the mysteries of the universe. With each new day, Kelvin's adventure continued, a testament to the enduring spirit of exploration and the unbreakable bonds of family and friendship in the wondrous world of BIORUTA.

Leaving the iridescent beauty of the Crystal Forest behind, Kelvin ventured into the Misty Highlands, an area enshrouded in a perpetual, gentle fog that lent an air of mystique to the rolling hills and meadows. The highlands were a place of quiet and contemplation, where the whispers of the wind seemed to carry old tales and secrets.

As he journeyed through the highlands, Kelvin encountered wandering minstrels, herders with their flocks, and solitary monks who had taken to the hills in search of peace and enlightenment. From each, he gathered stories and wisdom, each adding to his understanding of BIORUTA and its rich tapestry of life.

In a secluded valley within the highlands, Kelvin stumbled upon a hidden grove, a place of serenity where time seemed to stand still. The grove was filled with ancient trees, their branches forming a canopy above that filtered the light into a soft, dreamlike quality. In the center of the grove was a clear pool, its waters still and deep.

Drawn to the pool, Kelvin gazed into its depths. The water mirrored not only his own reflection but also shimmering images that seemed to hint at possible paths and futures. It was as if the pool were showing him the myriad ways his journey could unfold, each a different thread in the fabric of fate.

Leaving the grove with a sense of peace, Kelvin continued his travels across the highlands. The landscape gradually changed as he descended, leading him to the borders of the Echoing Valleys, a vast network of canyons known for their acoustic properties, where even the slightest sound could be carried for miles.

In the Echoing Valleys, Kelvin's journey took a turn towards the introspective. The echoes of his own footsteps and the sound of his breath reminded him of the journey's solitude and the distance he had traveled. Yet, these echoes also spoke of persistence and resilience, reinforcing his determination to find his family and uncover the truth of their disappearance.

Throughout his time in the valleys, Kelvin encountered nomadic tribes who treated him with kindness and shared their knowledge of the land. They spoke of the valleys as sacred places, where one could hear the whispers of the earth and the songs of the ancestors.

As Kelvin journeyed out of the Echoing Valleys, he found himself at the foot of the Great Volcanic Range, a series of dormant and active volcanoes that marked a dramatic change in the landscape. The ground here was rich and fertile, fed by the volcanic soil, and the air carried a hint of sulfur and minerals.

Climbing the slopes of one of the more gentle volcanoes, Kelvin discovered a network of hot springs and geysers, natural wonders that drew visitors from across BIORUTA. The springs were places of healing and rejuvenation, and Kelvin took the time to rest, allowing the warm waters to soothe his weary muscles.

Atop the volcanic range, Kelvin had a panoramic view of BIORUTA, a vista that stretched from the misty highlands to the shimmering sea. It was a moment of reflection, a time to contemplate the journey he had undertaken. He had traversed diverse landscapes, met a myriad of creatures, and learned the deep secrets of the planet. Each experience had shaped him, teaching him about the world and about himself.

As Kelvin descended from the volcanic range, his heart was filled with a mixture of anticipation and resolve. His journey had taken him across the length and breadth of BIORUTA, each step revealing new wonders and deepening his connection to the planet. The quest to find his family had become a journey of discovery and growth, a testament to the enduring power of hope and the spirit of adventure.

In the vast and wondrous world of BIORUTA, Kelvin's journey continued, a quest that was both personal and profound, leading him ever onward in his search for his family and the deeper truths of the universe.

With the Great Volcanic Range behind him, Kelvin ventured into the region known as the Twilight Marshes. This area was a sprawling wetland, where the light of day and night seemed to blend, creating an ever-present twilight. The marshes were home to a diverse array of wildlife, and the air was filled with the sounds of chirping frogs, buzzing insects, and the gentle rustle of the wind through the reeds.

Navigating the marshes was challenging, as the ground was often soft and treacherous. Kelvin carefully made his way across, using the sturdy paths provided by nature – fallen logs, solid ground patches, and shallow waters. The marshes were a test of his agility and patience, but they also held a unique beauty, with their reflective pools mirroring the sky and the lush greenery providing a serene backdrop.

In the heart of the Twilight Marshes, Kelvin encountered a wise old heron who spoke of the cycles of nature and the ebb and flow of life. The heron, with its calm demeanor and insightful words, offered Kelvin a different perspective on his journey. "Each step you take is a ripple in the water, affecting everything around you. Your journey is more than a path through the world; it's a journey through the layers of life itself," the heron said in a slow, deliberate tone.

These words struck a chord in Kelvin, making him reflect on the impact of his journey, not just on himself but on the world around him. He realized that his quest was interconnected with the lives of all he had met and the places he had visited.

Leaving the marshes, Kelvin found himself at the edge of the Starlit Plains, an expansive grassland that stretched out under the open sky. At night, the plains were aglow with the light of a million stars, creating a celestial spectacle on the ground.

As he journeyed across the Starlit Plains, Kelvin marveled at the vastness of the open space. The plains were a place of freedom and wonder, where he could see for miles and where the sky felt close enough to touch. Here, he encountered nomadic tribes who roamed the plains, following the stars and the seasons. They shared stories of the sky and the constellations, teaching Kelvin how to read the night sky and find his way by the stars.

Each night on the plains, Kelvin would look up at the stars, thinking of his family and wondering if they too were looking up at the same sky. The stars became his companions, guiding him across the open land and filling him with a sense of wonder and hope.

After crossing the Starlit Plains, Kelvin's path led him to the Edge of the World, a breathtaking cliff that overlooked the vast ocean. Standing at the edge, he felt a sense of awe at the magnitude of the world and his place in it. The ocean stretched out endlessly, its surface reflecting the sky and merging with the horizon.

At the Edge of the World, Kelvin took time to reflect on his journey. He had traversed diverse landscapes, encountered a myriad of beings, and learned about the deep interconnectedness of all life on BIORUTA. His journey had been a transformative experience, shaping him into a wiser, more resilient being.

As he gazed out at the ocean, Kelvin knew that his journey was far from over. There were still many mysteries to uncover and paths to explore. His quest to find his family was intertwined with a larger journey of discovery – a journey that spanned the wonders of BIORUTA and the mysteries of the cosmos.

With the ocean's vast expanse before him and the sky above, Kelvin stepped forward, ready to continue his adventure. His heart was filled with hope, and his spirit was undaunted. In the vast and wondrous world of BIORUTA, Kelvin's story continued, a tale of courage, hope, and the unbreakable bonds of family and friendship.

Kelvin's journey now took him along the rugged coastline, where the land met the sea in a symphony of waves crashing against cliffs and beaches. The coastal route was a new environment for Kelvin, offering him a different perspective of BIORUTA's diverse landscapes. Here, the air was filled with the scent of salt and the rhythmic sound of the ocean.

As he traveled, Kelvin met fishermen and sailors, each with their own stories of the sea – tales of mysterious islands, great storms, and creatures that dwelled in the depths. These stories captivated Kelvin, adding layers to his understanding of BIORUTA and its many mysteries.

One day, while exploring a cove hidden among the cliffs, Kelvin came across an old lighthouse, its beacon a guide for ships navigating the treacherous waters. The lighthouse keeper, an elderly man with a wealth of knowledge about the sea, shared with Kelvin the legends of the Lost Isles, a group of islands that appeared and disappeared with the tides and were said to hold ancient secrets.

Intrigued by the possibility that his family might have explored such mysterious places, Kelvin set out to find these elusive isles. With the help of the lighthouse keeper and a sturdy boat, Kelvin embarked on a journey across the waves, guided by the stars and the patterns of the tides.

The sea journey was a new adventure for Kelvin, filled with awe and challenges. He witnessed the majesty of the ocean, its vastness, and its power. He encountered dolphins and whales, who danced around the boat, and saw schools of fish that glittered like underwater stars.

After days at sea, Kelvin finally glimpsed the Lost Isles in the distance, emerging from the mist like a mirage. The islands were a wonder to behold, with lush forests, cascading waterfalls, and exotic wildlife. Exploring the islands, Kelvin found remnants of ancient civilizations – ruins overgrown with vines, stone carvings weathered by time, and hidden caves filled with old treasures.

On one of the islands, in a secluded glade, Kelvin discovered a stone tablet inscribed with ancient symbols. These symbols spoke of the alignment of stars and planets, echoing the celestial themes he had encountered throughout his journey. Kelvin felt a deep connection to these symbols, sensing that they were a key part of the puzzle surrounding his family's disappearance.

As the tide began to turn, signaling the time to leave, Kelvin reluctantly departed from the Lost Isles, taking with him memories and clues that would aid him in his quest. The sea had shown him a world of wonders and deepened his connection to the mysteries of BIORUTA.

Returning to the mainland, Kelvin continued his journey along the coastline, each step taking him closer to unravelling the mystery of his family's disappearance. His heart was filled with a mix of longing, hope, and determination. The journey had taught him resilience, the value of friendship, and the interconnectedness of all life.

Kelvin's quest had become more than a search for his family; it was a journey of discovery and growth, an exploration of the beautiful and mysterious world of BIORUTA. With the vast ocean behind him and the endless sky above, Kelvin's adventure continued, his spirit unbroken and his resolve unwavering. In the great tapestry of BIORUTA's history, Kelvin's story was being woven, a tale of courage, hope, and the enduring power of love and exploration.

Kelvin's journey next led him inland, towards the heart of BIORUTA, a region known for its lush valleys and tranquil rivers. This part of the planet was a stark contrast to the rugged coastline he had just traversed. Here, the land was gentle, with rolling hills and meadows blanketed in wildflowers. The rivers meandered through the landscape, their waters clear and teeming with life.

As he traveled through the valleys, Kelvin encountered communities of diverse beings living in harmony with nature. They were farmers, artisans, and healers, each contributing to the wellbeing of their community. These encounters enriched Kelvin's understanding of the different ways life thrived on BIORUTA, and he found himself learning about agriculture, herbalism, and the art of crafting from natural materials.

In one particular village, nestled by a serene river, Kelvin met a group of elders who were custodians of ancient lore. They shared with him stories of the land, tales of the seasons, and the cycles of life. The elders spoke of a time long ago when the balance of nature had shifted, leading to great changes across BIORUTA. These stories echoed the themes Kelvin had heard throughout his journey – of balance, harmony, and the interconnectedness of all things.

Further into the heartland, Kelvin discovered the Orchard of Whispers, an ancient grove known for its fruit trees that bore not only fruit but also wisdom. It was said that those who listened closely could hear the trees whispering secrets and ancient truths. As Kelvin walked among the trees, he felt a sense of calm and clarity. The whispers of the trees, though faint, seemed to speak directly to his heart, offering guidance and reassurance.

The Orchard of Whispers became a place of reflection for Kelvin. He spent days there, contemplating his journey, the lessons he had learned, and the path that lay ahead. He realized that his search for his family had transformed him in ways he could never have imagined. He had become a seeker of knowledge, a friend to many, and a guardian of the secrets he had uncovered.

Leaving the orchard, Kelvin journeyed on, his spirit enriched by the experiences and connections he had made. He crossed verdant plains, hiked through dense forests, and traversed serene meadows, each landscape revealing its own beauty and secrets.

As he journeyed, Kelvin often looked to the skies, reminded of the cosmic forces that influenced BIORUTA. He had learned much about the planet's connection to the stars and the celestial events that shaped its destiny. These celestial themes had become a guiding light in his quest, leading him to places and encounters that were intertwined with the mysteries of the universe.

Kelvin's journey had taken him across the breadth of BIORUTA, through diverse ecosystems and communities, each with its own story and wisdom. He had grown in knowledge and understanding, his quest evolving into a journey of discovery and connection.

As he continued his journey through the heart of BIORUTA, Kelvin knew that each step brought him closer to finding his family and unraveling the greater mysteries of the planet. His adventure was a testament to the enduring power of hope and the unbreakable bonds of family. In the vast and wondrous world of BIORUTA, Kelvin's story continued, a tale of exploration, discovery, and the enduring spirit of adventure.

Kelvin's path led him next to the Singing Hills, an enchanting region where the wind created melodies as it passed through the valleys and crests. This natural music gave the area a mystical quality, making it a popular destination for poets, artists, and dreamers from across BIORUTA.

As he roamed the Singing Hills, Kelvin found himself inspired by the melodic landscape. The music of the wind seemed to speak to his soul, encouraging him to keep moving forward in his quest. In these hills, he met fellow travelers who shared their stories and joined him around campfires at night, exchanging tales and songs under the stars.

One night, while gazing at the starlit sky, Kelvin met an old astronomer who told him about the constellations and their stories. The astronomer spoke of a rare celestial event that was due to occur soon, an event that Kelvin realized might be linked to his family's disappearance. This revelation filled him with a renewed sense of urgency and purpose.

Leaving the Singing Hills, Kelvin ventured into the Realm of Shadows, a mysterious forest where the trees were so dense that they blotted out much of the light. This realm was rumored to be home to ancient spirits and hidden knowledge. Navigating through the dimly lit forest, Kelvin felt as though he was walking through another world, one that teemed with unseen presences and ancient magic.

In the heart of the Realm of Shadows, Kelvin encountered a wise old tree spirit who spoke of the balance between light and darkness, and the importance of embracing both. The spirit offered Kelvin guidance, hinting that the answers he sought might not be found in the light alone but in understanding the darkness as well.

With new insights, Kelvin continued his journey, the landscape gradually giving way to the Radiant Meadows, a vast expanse of fields ablaze with bioluminescent flowers that glowed in the twilight. The meadows were a spectacle of colors and light, creating a landscape that seemed otherworldly.

Here in the Radiant Meadows, Kelvin encountered a group of nature sprites who danced and played among the flowers. They were joyful beings, full of laughter and light, and they reminded Kelvin of the beauty and wonder that existed in the world, despite the challenges and uncertainties of his quest.

Each region of BIORUTA that Kelvin explored added to his understanding of the planet and its intricate web of life. He learned from every being he met, each one contributing to his growing knowledge of the world and its mysteries.

As he journeyed through the Radiant Meadows, Kelvin felt a deep connection to BIORUTA and its many inhabitants. His quest to find his family had led him on an extraordinary journey, one that had taught him about the complexities and wonders of the planet. He knew that each step brought him closer to finding his family and to understanding the greater purpose of his journey.

Kelvin's adventure continued, a journey of discovery and growth in the vast and wondrous world of BIORUTA. His heart was full of hope, his spirit resilient, and his determination unwavering. In his quest, he had become more than a seeker; he had become a guardian of the mysteries and a storyteller of the planet's tales.

Beyond the Radiant Meadows, Kelvin's travels brought him to the Cascading Falls, a region where mighty rivers plunged over cliffs, creating mesmerizing waterfalls that echoed through the valleys. The area was a convergence of water and earth, symbolizing the flow and resilience of nature.

At the Cascading Falls, Kelvin encountered a community of water dwellers who lived in harmony with the rushing waters. They were skilled swimmers and divers, teaching Kelvin about the rhythms of the rivers and the life that thrived in and around them. From them, he learned about the interconnectedness of waterways and how they shaped the land and life of BIORUTA.

Following the course of the rivers, Kelvin's journey led him to the Great Basin, a vast wetland teeming with diverse ecosystems. In this sprawling expanse, he navigated through marshes, lakes, and rivers, each habitat revealing its own unique beauty and challenges.

In the heart of the Great Basin, Kelvin stumbled upon an ancient water temple, half-submerged and overgrown with aquatic plants. The temple was a relic from a bygone era, its walls inscribed with runes and symbols that spoke of water's importance in the cycle of life and the balance of nature.

Exploring the water temple, Kelvin felt a profound sense of connection to the past. The temple held secrets of ancient wisdom, a testament to the knowledge and reverence the old civilizations of BIORUTA had for the natural world.

Leaving the Great Basin, Kelvin found himself drawn to the Whispering Dunes, a vast desert that contrasted starkly with the lush wetlands he had just left. The dunes were a sea of sand, sculpted by the winds into ever-changing patterns. The desert was both beautiful and daunting, a reminder of the planet's diverse and dynamic nature.

In the Whispering Dunes, Kelvin experienced the solitude and vastness of the desert. He learned to navigate by the sun and stars, finding his way through the shifting sands. At night, the desert transformed, the cool air bringing relief from the day's heat and the sky displaying a breathtaking array of stars.

One clear night, while gazing at the stars, Kelvin met a group of desert astronomers who shared with him the ancient art of celestial navigation and the stories written in the night sky. Their knowledge of the stars deepened Kelvin's understanding of BIORUTA's place in the cosmos and the celestial forces that influenced its destiny.

Each step of Kelvin's journey through BIORUTA brought new experiences and insights. From the Cascading Falls to the Great Basin, from the Whispering Dunes to the starlit desert nights, he encountered the planet's many faces, each one revealing a piece of the grand puzzle he was trying to solve.

Kelvin's quest to find his family had evolved into a journey of understanding the intricate web of life that made up BIORUTA. His heart was filled with a blend of longing, hope, and awe, his spirit enriched by the wonders and wisdom of the planet. In his search for his family, Kelvin had become a wanderer, a learner, and a guardian of the planet's tales, each step a testament to the enduring power of hope and the unbreakable bonds of family in the magnificent world of BIORUTA.

Leaving the vast expanse of the Whispering Dunes behind, Kelvin journeyed towards the Northern Reaches, a region known for its rugged terrain and diverse wildlife. The Northern Reaches were a frontier of sorts, where the landscapes varied from dense forests to rocky outcrops, each area offering its own unique challenges and beauty.

As Kelvin traversed this region, he encountered a variety of creatures that called the Northern Reaches home. Majestic elk roamed the forests, while eagles soared high above the mountains. Each creature he met shared a piece of their story with him, adding to his understanding of the delicate balance of life in BIORUTA.

One of the most remarkable experiences in the Northern Reaches was Kelvin's encounter with a pack of wild wolves. These wolves were not just inhabitants of the region but guardians of its ancient secrets. They shared with Kelvin the lore of the land, tales of the spirits that watched over the forests and mountains, and the ancient rites that kept the balance of nature.

In the heart of the Northern Reaches, Kelvin discovered the Crystal Caverns, a network of underground tunnels illuminated by natural crystal formations. The crystals radiated a soft light, casting a magical glow on the walls of the caverns. Exploring these caverns, Kelvin felt as if he had stepped into a world of wonder and mystery.

The Crystal Caverns were not just natural wonders but also a repository of knowledge. The walls of the caverns were etched with markings and symbols that told stories of the planet's history, its connection to the cosmos, and the ancient civilizations that once thrived on BIORUTA.

As he journeyed deeper into the caverns, Kelvin came upon a crystal-clear underground lake. The surface of the lake was so still that it perfectly mirrored the ceiling of the cavern, creating an illusion of a starry sky below. Kelvin realized that the Crystal Caverns were a microcosm of BIORUTA itself, a blend of natural beauty and cosmic mystery.

Leaving the Crystal Caverns, Kelvin continued his journey through the Northern Reaches, each day bringing new discoveries and encounters. He learned to navigate the rugged terrain, to understand the language of the wind and the trees, and to respect the wildness of the land.

As he neared the end of the Northern Reaches, Kelvin found himself at the edge of the Aurora Forest, a mystical woodland known for its ethereal beauty. The forest was named after the auroras that frequently danced in the sky above, casting vibrant colors that illuminated the trees and the forest floor.

In the Aurora Forest, Kelvin experienced the magic of the auroras firsthand. The light show in the sky was mesmerizing, a celestial spectacle that filled him with awe and wonder. The forest under the auroras felt alive with energy, a place where the boundaries between the earthly and the celestial seemed to blur.

Kelvin's time in the Aurora Forest was a period of reflection and growth. He had traveled far and wide across BIORUTA, learning from its many inhabitants and uncovering the secrets of the planet. The journey had transformed him, shaping him into a being of wisdom and courage.

As he left the Aurora Forest, Kelvin knew that his journey was far from over. There were still many paths to explore, mysteries to unravel, and truths to discover. His quest to find his family had become a journey of discovery, a quest to understand the interconnectedness of all life on BIORUTA and the cosmic forces that shaped its destiny.

In the vast and wondrous world of BIORUTA, Kelvin's adventure continued, a journey of exploration, discovery, and the enduring spirit of adventure. His heart was filled with hope, his spirit resilient, and his determination unwavering. Kelvin's story was a testament to the enduring power of love and the unbreakable bonds of family in the magnificent tapestry of BIORUTA.

After leaving the Aurora Forest, Kelvin's path led him to the Mystic Glades, a serene and enchanting region where the flora and fauna seemed to be imbued with a subtle magic. The glades were a harmonious blend of natural beauty and mystical energy, a place where the air itself seemed to hum with an unseen power.

In the Mystic Glades, Kelvin encountered a community of druids who had a deep understanding of the natural world and its energies. They lived in harmony with the land, practicing ancient rituals that honored the cycles of nature and the spirits of the forest. The druids welcomed Kelvin and shared their wisdom with him, teaching him about the medicinal properties of plants and the hidden language of trees.

One of the druids, an elder named Elowen, took a special interest in Kelvin's quest. She listened intently to his story, her eyes reflecting a deep knowledge and empathy. "Your journey is a reflection of the journey of life itself," she told him. "It is filled with twists and turns, shadows and light, but each step is a step towards understanding."

Elowen guided Kelvin through the Mystic Glades, showing him the sacred sites that were vital to the balance of the region. She spoke of the interconnectedness of all things, how the health of one part of the ecosystem affected the whole. Kelvin realized that his journey was not just a physical quest, but also a spiritual one.

Leaving the Mystic Glades, Kelvin journeyed towards the Sunlit Peaks, a majestic mountain range that was bathed in sunlight. The peaks were home to a diverse array of wildlife and offered breathtaking views of BIORUTA. As he climbed the rugged paths, Kelvin felt a sense of accomplishment and awe. The world below seemed vast and endless, a tapestry of landscapes that he had traversed in his quest.

Atop the Sunlit Peaks, Kelvin met a group of monks who had devoted their lives to studying the skies and the movements of the celestial bodies. They offered Kelvin a different perspective on his journey, one that was aligned with the cosmos. They spoke of the stars as guides and teachers, each constellation telling a story that had been passed down through generations.

The monks shared with Kelvin the legend of the Starborn, beings who were said to have descended from the stars to guide and protect BIORUTA. Kelvin wondered if his family's disappearance was connected to this ancient legend, a thought that filled him with both curiosity and hope.

Descending from the Sunlit Peaks, Kelvin's journey took him to the Edge of the Horizon, a vast plain where the sky and land seemed to merge. Here, the landscape was open and endless, offering a sense of freedom and possibility. Kelvin felt as though he was walking towards the edge of the world, each step taking him closer to the unknown.

The Edge of the Horizon was a place of reflection and contemplation. Kelvin looked back on his journey, marveling at how far he had come and how much he had learned. He had crossed diverse regions, met incredible beings, and uncovered the mysteries and wonders of BIORUTA. His quest had become a journey of discovery, not just of his family, but of himself and the world around him.

As Kelvin stood at the Edge of the Horizon, gazing out at the vast expanse before him, he knew that his adventure was far from over. There were still many paths to explore, secrets to uncover, and connections to be made. His journey had taught him about the beauty and complexity of life, the interconnectedness of all things, and the enduring power of hope and love.

In the magnificent world of BIORUTA, Kelvin's story continued, a tale of exploration, discovery, and the unbreakable bonds of family and friendship. His heart was full of hope, his spirit unbroken, and his resolve stronger than ever. Kelvin's journey was a testament to the enduring spirit of adventure and the quest for understanding in the vast and wondrous tapestry of life.

Continuing his journey from the Edge of the Horizon, Kelvin ventured into the Veiled Valley, a mystical region enshrouded in a perpetual mist that gave it an ethereal quality. The valley was a place of legend, known for its hidden mysteries and ancient energies. As he moved through the mist, Kelvin felt as if he were walking through a dream, the landscape around him both familiar and otherworldly.

In the Veiled Valley, Kelvin encountered a tribe of seers, beings who were said to possess the gift of foresight. The seers lived in harmony with the valley's mystical energies, their eyes seemingly able to pierce through the veils of time and space. Intrigued by Kelvin's quest, they offered to read the signs and omens that surrounded his journey.

Sitting around a fire, under a canopy of stars barely visible through the mist, the seers cast their runes and read the patterns in the smoke. They spoke of a convergence of paths, a meeting of destinies that was entwined with Kelvin's search for his family. They warned him of challenges ahead but also foretold of hope and guidance from unexpected sources.

Heartened by the seers' words, Kelvin continued his exploration of the valley, discovering ancient ruins and hidden groves that seemed untouched by time. Each place he visited in the Veiled Valley felt imbued with a sense of purpose, as if the very stones and trees were aware of his quest and were guiding him forward.

Leaving the mystical embrace of the Veiled Valley, Kelvin found himself journeying towards the Celestial Gardens, a region famed for its extraordinary beauty and lush landscapes. The gardens were a living tapestry of flowers, trees, and winding streams, each element carefully tended to create a harmony between nature and art.

In the Celestial Gardens, Kelvin was struck by the sheer diversity of life that thrived in the carefully curated ecosystems. Here, he met gardeners and botanists who shared with him their knowledge of the flora, each plant and flower having its own story and significance. The gardens were more than a place of beauty; they were a testament to the balance between nature and the careful hand of nurturing.

Among the vibrant paths of the Celestial Gardens, Kelvin found a sense of peace. The beauty of the place reminded him of the inherent wonder of BIORUTA and its many mysteries. It was a reminder that his journey, with all its trials and discoveries, was a part of the planet's rich tapestry of life.

With the colors and scents of the Celestial Gardens still lingering in his senses, Kelvin set out once again, his journey taking him to the Echoing Mountains, a range of towering peaks known for their acoustic phenomena. The mountains were said to carry sounds for miles, creating a symphony of echoes that resonated through the valleys.

Climbing the steep paths of the Echoing Mountains, Kelvin felt as though he were ascending into the very heart of BIORUTA's mysteries. The mountains were a place of challenge and revelation, their peaks offering breathtaking views and their echoes carrying the whispers of the planet's ancient past.

At the summit of one of the highest peaks, Kelvin paused to take in the view. Below him, the landscapes he had traversed stretched out in a mosaic of colors and textures, each region a chapter in his ongoing journey. From the Mystic Glades to the Singing Hills, from the Crystal Caverns to the Celestial Gardens, each step had brought him closer to understanding the depth and complexity of BIORUTA.

As he stood on the peak, Kelvin realized that his journey was more than a search for his family. It was a quest for understanding the interconnectedness of life, the mysteries of the cosmos, and his own place within the grand scheme of existence. With each new discovery, each new connection, Kelvin was weaving his own story into the fabric of BIORUTA's history.

Descending from the Echoing Mountains, Kelvin's heart was filled with a sense of purpose and determination. His journey would continue, each step a part of the greater journey that connected him to the heart and soul of BIORUTA. In the vast and wondrous world of BIORUTA, Kelvin's adventure continued, a tale of exploration, discovery, and the enduring bonds of love and friendship.

From the majestic heights of the Echoing Mountains, Kelvin's journey brought him to the serene shores of the Sapphire Lakes, a series of interconnected lakes known for their crystal-clear waters and vibrant aquatic life. The lakes were a tranquil oasis, a stark contrast to the ruggedness of the mountains he had just left.

As he explored the shores and forests surrounding the lakes, Kelvin encountered a variety of creatures that thrived in this aquatic paradise. He met otters who playfully slid down the muddy banks, herons that stood like sentinels in the shallow waters, and schools of fish that shimmered beneath the surface like living jewels.

In the Sapphire Lakes, Kelvin learned about the importance of water in the ecosystem and the delicate balance that needed to be maintained to ensure the health and prosperity of the aquatic life. The lakes were a reminder of the interconnectedness of all ecosystems on BIORUTA and the role each habitat played in the greater environmental tapestry.

One evening, by the gentle glow of a campfire near the water's edge, Kelvin met an old fisherman who shared tales of the lakes and the legends that surrounded them. The fisherman spoke of a mythical creature that was said to dwell in the deepest lake, a guardian of the waters and a symbol of the lakes' ancient magic.

Intrigued by these legends, Kelvin decided to spend some time by the lakes, immersing himself in the beauty and tranquility of the area. He would sit by the water for hours, watching the play of light on the surface and feeling a deep sense of peace and connection with the natural world.

Leaving the Sapphire Lakes, Kelvin ventured into the Twilight Woods, a dense forest where the light seemed to be perpetually dim, creating an atmosphere of mystery and enchantment. The woods were known for their ancient trees, some of which were said to be as old as BIORUTA itself.

The Twilight Woods were a place of quiet and introspection. As Kelvin wandered through the thick underbrush and overgrown paths, he felt as though he were walking through a living history, each tree and stone holding stories of the past. The forest had a timeless quality, a reminder of the enduring nature of life and the cycles of growth and decay.

In the heart of the woods, Kelvin came upon an old stone well, covered in moss and ivy. Legend had it that the well was a source of wisdom, its waters holding the reflections of truth. Drawn to the well, Kelvin peered into its depths, finding not water, but a mirror-like surface that seemed to gaze back into his soul.

As he looked into the well, Kelvin saw not just his reflection, but glimpses of his journey – the places he had visited, the beings he had met, and the experiences he had encountered. The well's reflections were a mosaic of his quest, each piece a part of the greater journey he was on.

Leaving the Twilight Woods, Kelvin felt a renewed sense of purpose. His journey through BIORUTA had taken him through varied and wondrous landscapes, each with its own beauty and secrets. From the Sapphire Lakes to the Twilight Woods, from the Echoing Mountains to the Mystic Glades, each step had been a step towards understanding the complexity and beauty of the world.

As he continued his journey, Kelvin knew that the path ahead would bring new challenges and discoveries. His quest to find his family was intertwined with a deeper quest – a quest to understand the interconnectedness of life, the mysteries of the cosmos, and his own place within the tapestry of BIORUTA. In the vast and wondrous world of BIORUTA, Kelvin's adventure continued, a journey of exploration, discovery, and the enduring spirit of hope and love.

Kelvin's path next took him to the Rolling Meadows, a vast expanse of open land dotted with wildflowers and gentle hills. The meadows were a vibrant canvas of colors, alive with the buzzing of bees, the fluttering of butterflies, and the songs of birds. This landscape offered a sense of freedom and space, a place where the sky seemed to join the earth in a seamless horizon.

In the Rolling Meadows, Kelvin encountered shepherds tending to their flocks and travelers passing through on their journeys. Each person he met shared stories of their lives and experiences, enriching Kelvin's understanding of the diversity of life on BIORUTA. The meadows were a crossroads of sorts, a place where paths intersected and stories intertwined.

One clear night, while camping under the stars in the meadows, Kelvin met a group of stargazers. They showed him how to identify constellations and shared legends written in the night sky. The stargazers spoke of a cosmic event that was approaching, a convergence of celestial bodies that occurred once in a millennium. Kelvin listened intently, wondering if this event was connected to his family's disappearance.

Leaving the Rolling Meadows, Kelvin journeyed to the Ashen Plains, a stark landscape shaped by ancient volcanic activity. The plains were a contrast of blackened soil and regrowth, a testament to nature's resilience and ability to adapt and thrive even in the aftermath of upheaval.

In the Ashen Plains, Kelvin learned about the cycles of destruction and renewal, how the land had been reshaped by the forces of nature over countless centuries. The plains were a reminder of the ever-changing nature of the world, the constant ebb and flow of creation and transformation.

Crossing the plains, Kelvin arrived at the Pillars of Time, a series of towering rock formations that were said to be as old as BIORUTA itself. The pillars stood as silent sentinels, weathered by time and the elements. Carvings and symbols adorned their surfaces, each telling a story of the planet's history and the civilizations that had once thrived there.

Among the Pillars of Time, Kelvin felt a deep connection to the past. He traced his fingers over the ancient carvings, pondering the lives and stories of those who had come before him. The pillars were a bridge between the past and present, a physical representation of BIORUTA's long and storied history.

Leaving the Pillars of Time, Kelvin's journey took him to the Azure Highlands, a region of breathtaking beauty with rolling hills, pristine lakes, and a panorama of the skies. The highlands were a place of clarity and perspective, where one could gaze upon the vastness of BIORUTA and see the interconnectedness of all its regions.

In the Azure Highlands, Kelvin encountered a community of philosophers and thinkers who gathered to discuss the mysteries of life and the universe. They welcomed Kelvin into their discussions, intrigued by his journey and the wisdom he had gained along the way. The conversations he had in the highlands expanded his understanding of his place in the world and the larger cosmic tapestry.

As he left the Azure Highlands, Kelvin realized how much he had grown and evolved since the beginning of his journey. He had traversed diverse landscapes, encountered a myriad of beings, and learned about the deep connections that bound the planet together. His quest to find his family had become a journey of discovery, a quest to understand the mysteries of BIORUTA and the cosmos.

In the vast and wondrous world of BIORUTA, Kelvin's adventure continued, a tale of exploration, discovery, and the unbreakable bonds of love and friendship. His heart was filled with hope, his spirit resilient, and his determination stronger than ever. Kelvin's story was a testament to the enduring power of exploration and the quest for understanding in the magnificent tapestry of life.

From the Azure Highlands, Kelvin ventured into the Whispering Forest, a vast expanse of ancient trees known for their ability to seemingly communicate with each other through the rustling of leaves. The forest had an aura of wisdom and timelessness, each tree a witness to the ages that had passed. Walking through the forest, Kelvin felt as if he was being watched by ancient, knowing eyes.

The Whispering Forest was a sanctuary for many creatures, some of which were rarely seen elsewhere in BIORUTA. Enigmatic and elusive, they moved through the forest with a grace that spoke of their deep connection to this ancient place. Kelvin encountered wise owls, nimble deer, and even glimpsed what he thought might be a spirit of the forest, a being of light and shadow that disappeared as quickly as it appeared.

In this mystical forest, Kelvin stumbled upon an old hermit, a being who had lived in the forest for so long that they seemed to have become a part of it. The hermit spoke in riddles and parables, but each word was laden with meaning and wisdom. Kelvin spent several days with the hermit, absorbing the teachings and gaining insights into the deeper mysteries of life and nature.

Leaving the Whispering Forest, Kelvin found himself at the foothills of the Great Divide, a massive mountain range that stretched as far as the eye could see, its peaks shrouded in clouds. The mountains were a formidable barrier, but also a gateway to new lands and experiences. Kelvin began the arduous journey of scaling the peaks, each step taking him higher into the realm of the clouds.

Atop the Great Divide, Kelvin was met with a sight that took his breath away. Below him lay BIORUTA in all its splendor, a mosaic of every landscape he had traversed, each part integral to the whole. From this vantage point, Kelvin saw not just a planet, but a living, breathing entity of which he was a part.

The descent from the Great Divide brought Kelvin to the Valley of Shadows, a place of contrast where light and darkness interplayed, creating a landscape both foreboding and beautiful. The valley was a test of Kelvin's courage, as he navigated through the shadows, learning to see not just with his eyes, but with his heart.

Emerging from the Valley of Shadows, Kelvin journeyed into the Fields of Eternity, vast plains where time seemed to stand still. The fields were endless, their golden grasses swaying in the gentle breeze under an unchanging sky. Here, Kelvin found a tranquility that soothed his weary soul, a peaceful respite from the rigors of his journey.

As he lay in the Fields of Eternity, gazing up at the sky, Kelvin reflected on his journey. He had traveled through the myriad landscapes of BIORUTA, met its many inhabitants, and learned from each encounter and experience. His quest to find his family had become a journey of discovery, revealing the interconnectedness of all life and the mysteries of the universe.

In the vast and wondrous world of BIORUTA, Kelvin's adventure continued, a tale of exploration, discovery, and the unbreakable bonds of love and friendship. His heart was filled with hope, his spirit unbroken, and his resolve stronger than ever. Kelvin's story was a testament to the enduring spirit of adventure and the quest for understanding in the magnificent tapestry of life.

Kelvin's journey then led him to the Enchanted Canyons, a network of deep and winding gorges that carved through the heart of BIORUTA. The canyons were a marvel of natural architecture, with towering rock walls that changed color with the light of the sun. The echoes of the canyons carried the sound of rushing water from the rivers that flowed at their base, creating a symphony of nature's music.

As he navigated through the Enchanted Canyons, Kelvin encountered a diverse array of flora and fauna, each uniquely adapted to the canyon environment. He marveled at the agility of the mountain goats on the cliffs and the grace of the eagles soaring above. The canyons were a place of rugged beauty, offering a new perspective on the resilience and diversity of life.

In one of the canyons, Kelvin discovered ancient petroglyphs, carved into the rock faces by the early inhabitants of BIORUTA. These carvings told stories of the stars, the sun, and the moon, and of the people's deep connection to the land and the cosmos. Kelvin realized that every part of BIORUTA, including its very rocks and rivers, had a story to tell.

Exiting the canyons, Kelvin found himself in the Region of Mists, an area perpetually shrouded in a soft, ethereal fog. The mists gave the landscape a dreamlike quality, blurring the lines between reality and imagination. In this mystical region, Kelvin felt as if he was walking through the pages of a fairy tale.

The Region of Mists was home to elusive creatures and beings of legend. Kelvin heard tales of sprites that danced in the fog and of wise creatures that only appeared to those who were truly seeking knowledge. His time in the mists was filled with wonder and a sense of otherworldly magic.

Journeying onward, Kelvin arrived at the banks of the Great Serpent River, a mighty waterway that snaked across BIORUTA, connecting many of the regions he had traversed. The river was a lifeline of the planet, supporting an abundance of life along its banks and in its waters.

Traveling alongside the river, Kelvin experienced the ebb and flow of the water, the cycle of life that the river sustained. He met fishermen and river folk who shared their stories and their ways of life with him. The river was a symbol of continuity and change, its waters a reflection of the journey Kelvin was on.

As the Great Serpent River flowed into the Sea of Tranquility, Kelvin stood on the shores, looking out at the vast expanse of water that stretched to the horizon. The sea was a mirror of the sky, its surface reflecting the clouds and the colors of the sunset. Here, at the edge of the sea, Kelvin felt a deep connection to BIORUTA and its endless cycle of life.

Kelvin's journey through BIORUTA had been a journey through time and space, through landscapes of immense beauty and diversity. He had learned from the land, the water, the sky, and the many beings that called the planet home. His quest to find his family had evolved into a quest to understand the interconnectedness of all life and the mysteries of the cosmos.

In the vast and wondrous world of BIORUTA, Kelvin's adventure continued, a tale of exploration, discovery, and the enduring bonds of love and friendship. His heart was filled with hope, his spirit unbroken, and his determination stronger than ever. Kelvin's story was a testament to the enduring spirit of adventure and the quest for understanding in the magnificent tapestry of life.

Leaving the Sea of Tranquility, Kelvin ventured into the Forgotten Woods, an ancient forest that seemed untouched by time. The woods were dense and shadowy, with towering trees that whispered secrets of the ages. Here, Kelvin felt as though he had stepped into a realm where the past lingered, a place that held memories of the old world.

In the Forgotten Woods, Kelvin encountered enigmatic woodland creatures and spirits of nature. They shared with him ancient lore and tales of the forest, speaking of times when the woods were revered as sacred ground. Walking through this ancient place, Kelvin felt a profound respect for the natural world and its timeless cycles.

Deep within the Forgotten Woods, Kelvin found a hidden glen that radiated a gentle, soothing energy. In the center of the glen was an ancient tree, larger and older than any he had seen before. The tree seemed to be the heart of the forest, its roots delving deep into the earth and its branches reaching high into the sky. Kelvin sensed that the tree was a guardian of the woods, a keeper of its history and wisdom.

Leaving the Forgotten Woods, Kelvin's path led him to the Sunken Valleys, a series of lush, verdant valleys that lay hidden between steep cliffs. The valleys were a paradise of flora and fauna, a vibrant ecosystem teeming with life. The air was filled with the fragrance of flowers and the melodies of birdsong, creating a symphony of nature's beauty.

In the Sunken Valleys, Kelvin discovered communities of beings who lived in harmony with their surroundings. They cultivated the land with care, ensuring that the balance of nature was maintained. From these communities, Kelvin learned about sustainable living and the importance of nurturing the environment. Their way of life was a testament to the coexistence of civilization and nature.

Continuing his journey, Kelvin found himself drawn to the Crystal Tundra, a vast expanse of icy plains and frozen lakes that glistened like diamonds under the sun. The tundra was a land of stark beauty, its icy landscapes offering a serene yet formidable environment.

In the Crystal Tundra, Kelvin braved the cold and navigated the icy terrain, finding beauty in its simplicity and silence. The tundra was a place of reflection and introspection, where the challenges of the environment demanded resilience and adaptation. Kelvin's time in the tundra taught him about the strength and endurance of life in even the harshest conditions.

Leaving the Crystal Tundra, Kelvin's journey brought him to the Gateway of Legends, an ancient structure that stood at the crossroads of BIORUTA's many regions. The gateway was a monumental arch, covered in carvings and inscriptions that told stories of the planet's history and mythology.

Standing before the Gateway of Legends, Kelvin realized that his journey had taken him through a living tapestry of BIORUTA's history, culture, and natural wonders. He had traversed landscapes of immense beauty, encountered beings of wisdom and magic, and learned about the delicate balance that sustained life on the planet.

As he passed through the gateway, Kelvin knew that his journey was far from over. There were still many paths to explore, mysteries to unravel, and connections to be made. His quest to find his family had become a journey of discovery, a quest to understand the interconnectedness of all life and the mysteries of the cosmos.

In the vast and wondrous world of BIORUTA, Kelvin's adventure continued, a tale of exploration, discovery, and the enduring bonds of love and friendship. His heart was filled with hope, his spirit unbroken, and his determination stronger than ever. Kelvin's story was a testament to the enduring spirit of adventure and the quest for understanding in the magnificent tapestry of life.

From the Gateway of Legends, Kelvin journeyed into the Land of Whispers, a mystical region where the air seemed to carry voices from the past. The land was dotted with ancient ruins and relics, each telling a story of civilizations long gone but not forgotten. The whispers were not just sounds but echoes of history and memory, resonating through the air.

As Kelvin explored the Land of Whispers, he encountered scholars and historians who had dedicated their lives to uncovering the secrets of the past. They spoke of great empires, wise rulers, and powerful sorcerers who had shaped the history of BIORUTA. From them, Kelvin learned about the rise and fall of civilizations, the flow of time, and the importance of remembering the past.

Deep within the Land of Whispers, Kelvin discovered a secluded library, hidden away in the ruins of an ancient city. The library was a treasure trove of knowledge, filled with scrolls and tomes that contained the collective wisdom of ages. Here, Kelvin spent days poring over texts, learning about the lore of BIORUTA, its myths, and its legends.

Leaving the Land of Whispers, Kelvin's path led him to the Fields of Twilight, a place where day and night seemed to merge, creating a perpetual dusk. The fields were serene and beautiful, with a calm that seemed to blanket the land. In this twilight realm, Kelvin felt a sense of tranquility and balance, a harmony between light and dark.

In the Fields of Twilight, Kelvin met with philosophers and poets who gathered to discuss the mysteries of existence and the nature of reality. Their conversations were deep and thought-provoking, challenging Kelvin to see the world in new ways. They spoke of the duality of existence, the interplay of opposites, and the unity that underlies all things.

Continuing his journey, Kelvin found himself in the Garden of Dreams, a surreal landscape where the boundaries between reality and imagination seemed to blur. The garden was a place of wonder and enchantment, with fantastical plants and creatures that defied explanation. Here, Kelvin's perceptions were challenged, and he learned to embrace the limitless possibilities of the imagination.

From the Garden of Dreams, Kelvin journeyed to the Mountains of Echoes, a range of towering peaks where the echoes of one's thoughts and dreams could be heard. Climbing the mountains was a journey of self-discovery, as Kelvin confronted his own fears, hopes, and desires, each echo a reflection of his inner world.

At the summit of the Mountains of Echoes, Kelvin had a panoramic view of BIORUTA, a vast and diverse world that he had traversed in his quest. He reflected on the journey he had undertaken, the lessons he had learned, and the connections he had made. The mountains were a place of insight and revelation, offering a perspective that encompassed the entirety of his journey.

Descending from the mountains, Kelvin's path took him to the Shores of Infinity, a coastline where the sea met the sky in an endless horizon. Here, the sound of the waves was a constant reminder of the infinite nature of the universe and the endless cycle of life.

Standing on the Shores of Infinity, Kelvin looked out at the vast expanse before him, his heart filled with a sense of wonder and an unquenchable thirst for knowledge and adventure. His journey had been a journey of discovery, a quest to understand the interconnectedness of all life and the mysteries of the cosmos.

In the vast and wondrous world of BIORUTA, Kelvin's adventure continued, a tale of exploration, discovery, and the enduring bonds of love and friendship. His heart was filled with hope, his spirit unbroken, and his determination stronger than ever. Kelvin's story was a testament to the enduring spirit of adventure and the quest for understanding in the magnificent tapestry of life.

Leaving the Shores of Infinity, Kelvin ventured into the Valley of Visions, a mystical place known for its ability to reveal truths and foretell futures. The valley was shrouded in a soft, ethereal light, and the air seemed charged with a palpable energy. Here, Kelvin encountered seers and oracles, beings gifted with the sight to peer beyond the veil of the present.

In the Valley of Visions, Kelvin sought guidance about his journey. The oracles, speaking in cryptic but profound language, offered him glimpses of potential paths and outcomes. They spoke of challenges yet to come and allies yet to be met, and of a destiny that was intricately woven with the tapestry of BIORUTA.

Emboldened by the oracles' insights, Kelvin continued his journey, which led him to the Frozen Expanse, a land of ice and snow that stretched to the horizon. The expanse was a testament to the planet's diversity, a stark landscape of frozen beauty. Here, Kelvin braved biting winds and snow-covered terrain, his resolve tested by the harsh conditions.

Despite the challenges, Kelvin found a unique beauty in the Frozen Expanse. The ice formations sparkled like jewels under the sun, and the night sky was clear and bright, filled with stars that shone with an otherworldly light. In this icy realm, Kelvin learned the value of perseverance and the strength that comes from facing and overcoming adversity.

Journeying onward, Kelvin arrived at the Oasis of Tranquility, a verdant haven in the midst of a vast desert. The oasis was a place of life and rejuvenation, with cool waters and lush vegetation providing a respite from the harsh desert outside its borders. Here, Kelvin rested and replenished his spirit, the tranquil environment a balm to his weary soul.

The Oasis of Tranquility was home to a diverse community of beings who lived in harmony with the land. They shared their knowledge of the desert with Kelvin, teaching him about the delicate balance of ecosystems and the importance of preserving the natural world. The oasis was a reminder of the resilience of life and the beauty that can be found even in the most unlikely places.

Leaving the oasis, Kelvin's journey took him through the Windswept Plateau, a vast, open landscape where the wind sculpted the earth into unique formations. The plateau was a place of freedom and expansiveness, where the sky seemed endless and the earth stretched out in all directions.

In the Windswept Plateau, Kelvin encountered nomadic tribes who traversed the landscape, following the rhythms of nature and the seasons. They welcomed Kelvin into their midst, sharing their culture and traditions with him. From them, Kelvin learned about the importance of community and the strength that comes from unity and cooperation.

As he left the Windswept Plateau, Kelvin realized that his journey through BIORUTA had been a transformative experience. He had traversed diverse landscapes, met an array of incredible beings, and learned profound lessons about life, nature, and the cosmos. His quest to find his family had evolved into a journey of self-discovery and understanding, a journey that had forever changed him.

In the vast and wondrous world of BIORUTA, Kelvin's adventure continued, a tale of exploration, discovery, and the enduring bonds of love and friendship. His heart was filled with hope, his spirit unbroken, and his determination stronger than ever. Kelvin's story was a testament to the enduring spirit of adventure and the quest for understanding in the magnificent tapestry of life.

From the Windswept Plateau, Kelvin's journey led him to the Luminous Archipelago, a group of islands surrounded by glowing waters, where bioluminescent organisms created a spectacle of light and color in the night sea. The archipelago was a place of wonder, its islands each possessing their own unique ecosystems and mysteries.

As Kelvin explored the Luminous Archipelago, he was struck by the diversity of life and the myriad ways in which it manifested. On one island, he discovered a rainforest teeming with vibrant flora and fauna, while another island was home to a peaceful community that had mastered the art of living in harmony with the sea.

The people of the archipelago shared their knowledge of the ocean and its creatures with Kelvin, teaching him about the importance of preserving the delicate balance of marine ecosystems. They showed him coral reefs teeming with life, underwater caves filled with ancient fossils, and open waters where majestic sea creatures roamed.

Leaving the Luminous Archipelago, Kelvin found himself drawn to the Celestial Highlands, a region where the mountains reached towards the heavens, and the night sky was so clear that it seemed one could touch the stars. The highlands were a place of beauty and isolation, offering a sense of peace and a connection to the greater universe.

In the Celestial Highlands, Kelvin encountered astronomers and sages who studied the stars and the mysteries of the cosmos. They shared with him their insights into the nature of the universe and the interconnectedness of all things. The highlands were a place of learning and discovery, where the mysteries of the cosmos were explored and revered.

From the highlands, Kelvin's journey took him to the Depths of Silence, an expansive desert where the sands stretched out endlessly, and the silence was so profound that it seemed to echo. The desert was a place of introspection and solitude, where one could reflect on the journey of life and find clarity amid the vastness.

In the Depths of Silence, Kelvin learned the value of stillness and the wisdom that can be found in solitude. He wandered the desert, feeling the ancient rhythms of the earth beneath his feet, and gazing at the endless sky above, contemplating the journey he had undertaken and the lessons he had learned.

Emerging from the desert, Kelvin arrived at the Garden of Time, a mystical place where it was said that time flowed differently. The garden was filled with plants and trees from different eras and regions, creating a tapestry of time and life. Here, Kelvin experienced a sense of timelessness, as if the past, present, and future were converging.

The Garden of Time was a place of reflection and understanding, where Kelvin could see the interconnectedness of his journey and the cyclical nature of life. He walked among the ancient trees and timeless flowers, feeling a deep connection to BIORUTA and its endless cycle of life.

As Kelvin left the Garden of Time, he felt a profound sense of completion and understanding. His journey through BIORUTA had taken him through a myriad of landscapes, each with its own beauty and secrets. He had met beings of wisdom and magic, learned about the delicate balance of ecosystems, and discovered the interconnectedness of all life.

In the vast and wondrous world of BIORUTA, Kelvin's adventure continued, a tale of exploration, discovery, and the enduring bonds of love and friendship. His heart was filled with hope, his spirit unbroken, and his determination stronger than ever. Kelvin's story was a testament to the enduring spirit of adventure and the quest for understanding in the magnificent tapestry of life.

Leaving the Garden of Time behind, Kelvin found his way to the Echoing Cliffs, a dramatic coastline where the sea met towering cliffs that echoed the sounds of the waves. The cliffs were a natural amphitheater, amplifying the symphony of the ocean and creating a mesmerizing soundscape.

As Kelvin journeyed along the cliff tops, he was captivated by the vastness of the ocean and the rhythmic music it created against the land. The Echoing Cliffs were a reminder of the planet's natural beauty and the powerful forces that shaped its landscapes. Here, Kelvin felt a deep sense of connection to BIORUTA and the natural world.

Continuing his travels, Kelvin ventured into the Forest of Whispers, a mystical woodland where it was said the trees could communicate with one another. The forest was a labyrinth of ancient trees and winding paths, with a quiet that was almost tangible. In this serene environment, Kelvin found himself listening to the subtle sounds of the forest, each rustle and whisper telling a story of the natural world.

In the heart of the Forest of Whispers, Kelvin encountered a wise old tree, known as the Sentinel of the Forest. This ancient being shared with Kelvin the history of the woodland and the creatures that called it home. The Sentinel spoke of the importance of protecting the forest and preserving its harmony. From this encounter, Kelvin gained a deeper appreciation for the delicate balance of ecosystems and the role each creature played in maintaining it.

Journeying onward, Kelvin arrived at the Cascades of Moonlight, a series of waterfalls that were illuminated by the moon, creating a breathtaking display of light and water. The cascades were a place of tranquility and beauty, where the water flowed with a grace and power that was both humbling and inspiring.

At the Cascades of Moonlight, Kelvin took time to rest and reflect on his journey. He thought about the many lands he had traversed, the diverse beings he had met, and the lessons he had learned. The cascades, with their serene beauty, were a perfect place for contemplation and renewal.

Leaving the cascades, Kelvin's path led him to the Plateau of Dreams, a highland region known for its stunning vistas and the clarity of its night skies. Here, the stars seemed close enough to touch, and the landscape was bathed in the gentle light of the moon and stars.

In the Plateau of Dreams, Kelvin encountered dreamweavers, mystical beings who could interpret the dreams and visions of those who visited their land. The dreamweavers helped Kelvin understand the deeper meanings of his own dreams, offering insights into his journey and the paths he had yet to explore.

From the Plateau of Dreams, Kelvin descended into the Valley of the Ancients, a sacred place where the history of BIORUTA seemed to come alive. The valley was home to ancient ruins, stone circles, and petroglyphs that told the story of the planet's past. Here, Kelvin felt as though he was walking through the pages of history, each step uncovering the layers of time.

The Valley of the Ancients was a place of learning and discovery. Kelvin explored the ruins, deciphering the symbols and carvings that adorned them. He learned about the ancient civilizations that had once thrived on BIORUTA, their cultures, their achievements, and their connection to the planet and the cosmos.

As he left the Valley of the Ancients, Kelvin realized that his journey through BIORUTA had been more than a quest to find his family. It had been a journey of discovery and understanding, a journey that had taught him about the interconnectedness of all life, the history of the planet, and the mysteries of the universe.

In the vast and wondrous world of BIORUTA, Kelvin's adventure continued, a tale of exploration, discovery, and the enduring bonds of love and friendship. His heart was filled with hope, his spirit unbroken, and his determination stronger than ever. Kelvin's story was a testament to the enduring spirit of adventure and the quest for understanding in the magnificent tapestry of life.

As the sun set on the Valley of the Ancients, casting a golden hue over the ancient stones, Kelvin stood at a crossroads. He had traversed the length and breadth of BIORUTA, each step a journey through time, nature, and the cosmos. His quest had grown into something greater than himself, a testament to the interconnectedness of life and the enduring spirit of adventure. With his heart full of hope and his spirit fueled by the countless wonders he had witnessed, Kelvin knew his journey was far from over. The search for his family was just one part of a larger tapestry, a story woven into the very fabric of BIORUTA. As the stars began to twinkle in the twilight sky, Kelvin stepped forward, ready to continue his quest, guided by the lessons of the past and the promise of the future.

CHAPTER 2: UNLIKELY ALLIES

Kelvin's journey brought him to the bustling city of Echoterra, a melting pot of cultures and species from across BIORUTA. It was here, in the vibrant market square, bustling with activity, that Kelvin's path crossed with Harper, a Martian trooper stationed on BIORUTA as part of an interplanetary exchange program.

Harper was unlike anyone Kelvin had met before. Clad in a suit of advanced Martian armor, she stood out in the crowd with her disciplined posture and alert gaze. Her mission on BIORUTA was to study the planet's unique ecosystems and establish diplomatic relations, but she found herself intrigued by the talking Golden Retriever seeking his family.

Their first encounter was one of curiosity and mutual respect. Kelvin, with his knowledge of BIORUTA's landscapes and cultures, and Harper, with her advanced technology and training, quickly realized that they could benefit from working together. Harper was particularly interested in the celestial phenomena Kelvin had learned about and saw a potential link to her own research.

As they embarked on their journey together, Kelvin and Harper formed an unlikely alliance. They traveled through the dense jungles of the Green Canopy, where Harper's technology helped them navigate the labyrinth of foliage and wildlife. Kelvin's instincts and knowledge of the natural world complemented Harper's skills, making them an effective team.

Their next destination was the Crystal Spire Mountains, a region of towering peaks and luminous crystal formations. Harper's interest in the area was more than academic; she suspected that the crystals might be similar to a rare mineral found on Mars, one with unique energy properties.

As they ascended the mountains, Kelvin and Harper faced various challenges, from navigating treacherous paths to encountering local wildlife. They learned to rely on each other's strengths – Kelvin's agility and understanding of the terrain, and Harper's technological expertise and tactical knowledge.

In the heart of the Crystal Spire Mountains, Kelvin and Harper discovered an ancient temple, half-buried in the snow. Inside, they found carvings and artifacts that hinted at a connection between BIORUTA and Mars, suggesting a shared history that predated their current civilizations.

This discovery was a breakthrough, hinting at a deeper mystery that tied Kelvin's quest to Harper's mission. It was clear that their journey together was about more than finding Kelvin's family – it was about uncovering the secrets of their planets and the connection that bound them.

As they left the Crystal Spire Mountains, Kelvin and Harper knew that their journey together was just beginning. With each step, they uncovered clues about Kelvin's family and the mysteries of BIORUTA and Mars. Their alliance had grown into a friendship, one forged in the spirit of discovery and a shared quest for knowledge.

In the vast and wondrous world of BIORUTA, Kelvin and Harper's adventure continued, a journey of exploration, discovery, and the forging of bonds that transcended worlds. Their story was a testament to the power of friendship, cooperation, and the unending quest for understanding in the magnificent tapestry of life.

As Kelvin and Harper journeyed on from the Crystal Spire Mountains, their next destination was the City of Mists, a mysterious place known for its perpetual fog and the secrets it concealed. The city was an ancient hub of knowledge and mysticism, where scholars and seers gathered to study the mysteries of BIORUTA.

Upon arriving in the City of Mists, Kelvin and Harper were greeted by a labyrinth of narrow streets and towering structures, all shrouded in a dense fog. The air was filled with the scents of exotic spices and the distant sound of chimes. It was a city that felt both ancient and alive, its secrets hidden in the mist.

Their first task in the city was to seek out an ancient library rumored to house texts and scrolls containing information about the celestial events and ancient connections between BIORUTA and Mars. Kelvin, with his keen sense of smell, and Harper, with her advanced navigational equipment, made their way through the winding streets to the heart of the city.

The library was a grand structure, its walls lined with shelves that reached the ceiling, filled with books and artifacts of ages past. Here, Kelvin and Harper delved into the ancient lore, uncovering tales of past civilizations, cosmic alignments, and legends of interstellar travel. The more they read, the more they realized that their journey was part of a much larger narrative, one that spanned galaxies and epochs.

As they studied, they were approached by an elder of the city, a wise and enigmatic figure who had heard of their quest. The elder offered them guidance, speaking of a hidden chamber beneath the city where the true secrets of the past were kept. Intrigued and eager to learn more, Kelvin and Harper followed the elder through secret passages and hidden doors, descending into the depths of the city.

In the hidden chamber, they found a room filled with ancient technology and star maps, the walls adorned with carvings that depicted celestial events and interplanetary connections. Here, Harper discovered a symbol that matched one from Martian lore, a symbol representing a bridge between worlds.

The discovery in the hidden chamber was a turning point in their journey. It suggested a shared history between BIORUTA and Mars, a connection that could explain the mysteries surrounding Kelvin's family and Harper's mission. The realization that their paths were intertwined with a larger cosmic story filled them with a sense of awe and a renewed determination to uncover the truth.

Leaving the City of Mists, Kelvin and Harper set out for the Verdant Expanse, a vast region of lush forests and abundant wildlife. Here, they hoped to find more clues about the ancient connection between their worlds and perhaps even a trail leading to Kelvin's family.

As they journeyed through the Verdant Expanse, the bond between Kelvin and Harper grew stronger. They faced challenges together, from navigating through dense undergrowth to encountering the wild creatures that called the forest home. Each obstacle they overcame brought them closer, forging a friendship that was built on trust, respect, and a shared sense of purpose.

In the heart of the Verdant Expanse, Kelvin and Harper stumbled upon an ancient stone circle, its stones aligned with celestial bodies. As they examined the site, they realized it was a star map, one that pointed to a specific alignment of planets, including Mars and BIORUTA. This alignment, they theorized, could be the key to unlocking the secrets of their shared past and the location of Kelvin's family.

Their journey through the Verdant Expanse concluded with more questions than answers, but with a clear direction for their next steps. Kelvin and Harper knew that their adventure was far from over. Together, they set out for their next destination, guided by the stars and the bond they had formed.

In the vast and wondrous world of BIORUTA, Kelvin and Harper's adventure continued, a journey of exploration, discovery, and the enduring bonds of friendship. Their story was a testament to the power of unity, the pursuit of knowledge, and the unending quest for understanding in the magnificent tapestry of life.

Continuing their journey, Kelvin and Harper set their sights on the Tidal Reaches, a coastal region where the sea's rhythms played a crucial role in shaping the landscape. The area was known for its expansive beaches and tidal pools that teemed with marine life, offering a different perspective on the planet's diverse ecosystems.

As they explored the Tidal Reaches, Kelvin and Harper encountered local communities who had adapted their lives to the ebb and flow of the tides. These communities shared their knowledge of the sea, teaching them about the delicate balance of marine ecosystems and the lore of the ocean. It was here that Harper collected valuable data on the planet's aquatic life, drawing parallels to her research on Martian water sources.

One significant discovery in the Tidal Reaches was an ancient underwater structure, revealed only during low tide. The structure bore symbols and markings similar to those they had found in the hidden chamber beneath the City of Mists. It suggested an ancient civilization that had a profound understanding of celestial patterns and their impact on the planet.

Kelvin and Harper's investigation of the structure led them to theorize that it was part of a network of ancient sites connected by a knowledge of cosmic events. This network, they hypothesized, could be the key to unlocking the mysteries of the connection between BIORUTA and Mars, and perhaps even the location of Kelvin's family.

With new clues in hand, Kelvin and Harper traveled inland to the Fading Plains, a region characterized by its vast, open landscapes and the phenomenon of shifting colors in the vegetation, a result of the unique mineral composition of the soil. The plains offered a stark beauty and a sense of endless space, where the sky touched the earth in a seamless horizon.

In the Fading Plains, they encountered migratory creatures whose patterns seemed to be influenced by the same celestial events they were researching. Kelvin and Harper spent time observing these patterns, noting the synchronization between the migrations and the cosmic cycles. This observation further supported their theory of an ancient, planet-wide understanding of the stars and their influence.

Their next destination was the Summit of Whispers, a high peak renowned for its clear skies and the clarity with which one could observe the stars and planets. The summit was a sacred place for astronomers and seekers of wisdom, offering an unobstructed view of the cosmos.

Atop the Summit of Whispers, Kelvin and Harper spent nights charting the stars, aligning their observations with the ancient maps and data they had collected. It was here that Harper made a breakthrough, discovering a pattern in the celestial alignments that corresponded with the historical events they had learned about in the ancient texts.

This discovery was a pivotal moment in their journey, linking the past events on BIORUTA with similar events recorded in Martian history. It suggested a shared legacy, a moment in time when their planets had been closely connected, perhaps by a civilization that had traveled between them.

As they descended from the Summit of Whispers, Kelvin and Harper knew that their journey was leading them towards a profound revelation. They were no longer just allies brought together by circumstance; they were partners in uncovering a cosmic mystery that spanned planets and ages.

Their adventure through the diverse landscapes of BIORUTA continued, each step bringing them closer to understanding the ancient connection between their worlds. In the vast and wondrous world of BIORUTA, Kelvin and Harper's journey of discovery, unity, and friendship continued, a testament to the enduring power of curiosity and the unbreakable bonds formed in the pursuit of knowledge.

With newfound determination fueled by their discoveries at the Summit of Whispers, Kelvin and Harper ventured towards the Nebula Forest, a mysterious and dense woodland where the trees emitted a soft, ethereal glow, akin to the distant nebulas seen in the night sky. The forest was a place of wonder, with its luminescent flora casting a surreal light on the paths beneath.

As they navigated through the Nebula Forest, Kelvin and Harper experienced a sense of otherworldliness. The light from the trees illuminated the forest in a kaleidoscope of colors, creating a landscape that felt like a living dream. It was here they hoped to find the Floris Arbor, an ancient tree rumored to be a living archive of BIORUTA's history.

In their search for the Floris Arbor, they encountered a variety of nocturnal creatures, each adapted to the unique environment of the forest. They met with a wise old owl, who spoke in riddles but pointed them in the direction of the ancient tree. After a journey deep into the heart of the forest, they finally came upon the Floris Arbor, a magnificent tree that towered above the rest, its bark shimmering with a light of its own.

The Floris Arbor was not just a tree; it was an entity, ancient and wise. Upon their approach, the tree's glow intensified, and its leaves rustled as if whispering secrets of the past. Kelvin and Harper felt a deep connection with the tree, sensing the knowledge it held. Using a combination of Harper's technological devices and Kelvin's intuitive connection with nature, they were able to communicate with the Floris Arbor.

The tree shared visions of the past, showing them glimpses of a time when BIORUTA and Mars were closely linked, with beings traveling between the two planets through means that defied current understanding. These visions aligned with the patterns they had observed in the stars and the ancient structures they had discovered.

Leaving the Nebula Forest with a deeper understanding of the ancient connection between their worlds, Kelvin and Harper set out for the Chasm of Echoes, a deep canyon known for its unusual acoustic properties. The chasm was a place where sound traveled in peculiar ways, creating echoes that could reveal hidden truths.

In the Chasm of Echoes, Kelvin and Harper conducted experiments, using the canyon's acoustics to unlock further secrets from the data they had collected. It was here that Harper made a crucial discovery – a frequency that resonated with the ancient structures they had found, suggesting a way to activate them, potentially opening pathways to uncovering more of their shared history.

With each step of their journey, Kelvin and Harper's bond grew stronger, their skills complementing each other in ways that neither could have anticipated. Kelvin's knowledge of BIORUTA's ecosystems and Harper's technological expertise were proving to be key in unraveling the mysteries of their planets' past.

Their journey continued, taking them across BIORUTA's varied and magical landscapes, each destination bringing them closer to understanding the ancient ties that bound their worlds. In the vast and wondrous world of BIORUTA, Kelvin and Harper's adventure was a journey of discovery, unity, and friendship, a testament to the power of collaboration and the enduring quest for knowledge.

Leaving the Chasm of Echoes with new insights, Kelvin and Harper journeyed towards the Plateau of Origins, a vast tableland rich with archaeological sites and ancient artifacts. This region was believed to hold key information about the earliest civilizations of BIORUTA, and perhaps clues to the planet's connection with Mars.

As they explored the plateau, Kelvin and Harper came across remnants of old settlements, stone structures, and intricate carvings that depicted celestial bodies and interplanetary travel. Among these ruins, they found fragments of a mineral similar to the one Harper had identified in the Crystal Spire Mountains, further solidifying the link between their two worlds.

The Plateau of Origins was also home to a group of historians and archaeologists, dedicated to uncovering the secrets of BIORUTA's past. Joining forces with these experts, Kelvin and Harper pieced together a timeline that suggested a period of significant interplanetary interaction, a time when BIORUTA and Mars may have shared knowledge, resources, and even inhabitants.

Their next destination was the Labyrinth of Reflections, a complex network of mirrored caverns that created an endless maze of reflections. Legend had it that these caverns were a test of truth and perception, revealing hidden truths to those who navigated them successfully.

Inside the labyrinth, Kelvin and Harper faced a challenging journey, as the reflections often led to confusion and disorientation. However, by relying on each other's strengths and perspectives, they navigated the maze, finding at its heart a chamber with a crystalline ceiling that reflected the stars. This chamber provided a map of sorts, aligning the stars with specific locations on BIORUTA, hinting at points of significant celestial influence.

With this star map as their guide, Kelvin and Harper set out for the Sea of Dunes, a vast desert with ever-shifting sands. Here, they hoped to find one of the locations indicated in the star map, a site that might hold further clues to the ancient connections between their worlds.

The journey across the Sea of Dunes was arduous, with the landscape constantly changing and the threat of sandstorms ever-present. Yet, amidst the challenges, the desert held a stark beauty, with its dunes reflecting the golden light of the sun by day and the silver glow of the stars by night.

In the heart of the desert, Kelvin and Harper discovered an ancient observatory, half-buried in the sand. This structure, aligned with specific celestial formations, seemed to be a part of a larger network, similar to what they had uncovered in the Plateau of Origins.

At the observatory, Harper's technical skills allowed them to activate ancient mechanisms, revealing a holographic projection of the solar system that included both BIORUTA and Mars. The projection showed alignments and connections that were previously unknown, suggesting that the ancient civilizations had a deep understanding of interplanetary dynamics.

Their findings in the Sea of Dunes marked a significant breakthrough in their quest. Kelvin and Harper realized that the story they were uncovering was not just of two separate planets but of a shared history, a legacy that spanned the stars.

With each new discovery, Kelvin and Harper's alliance grew stronger, their friendship deepened by the shared experiences and the mysteries they were unraveling together. In the vast and wondrous world of BIORUTA, their journey of discovery continued, a testament to the power of collaboration, curiosity, and the enduring bonds formed in the pursuit of a greater understanding.

Energized by the revelations at the Sea of Dunes, Kelvin and Harper set their course for the Verdant Canopy, an expansive rainforest known for its biodiversity and the ancient secrets it held. The canopy was a dense network of towering trees, vibrant flora, and diverse fauna, a testament to the richness of life on BIORUTA.

As they journeyed through the Verdant Canopy, they encountered numerous species, some of which were unique to this part of the planet. Harper's interest in the ecosystem was piqued by the remarkable adaptations of these creatures, while Kelvin was fascinated by the intricate balance of life within the forest. Their exploration led them to discover a hidden grove, where they found carvings on the trees that mirrored the symbols they had seen in the Sea of Dunes and the Plateau of Origins.

Deep within the rainforest, they stumbled upon an ancient temple, overgrown with vines and moss. The temple was a relic of a bygone era, its architecture suggesting a civilization that had a profound understanding of both the planet and the stars. Inside the temple, they found a series of murals depicting the relationship between BIORUTA and Mars, including images of travel between the two planets.

Kelvin and Harper's findings in the Verdant Canopy added another layer to the unfolding mystery of the ancient connection between their worlds. They hypothesized that the rainforest might have been a central hub for the ancient civilization, a place of knowledge and a gateway between worlds.

Their next destination was the Peaks of Solitude, a series of high mountains known for their serene beauty and the clarity of the air. The journey to the peaks was challenging, but the view from the top offered a new perspective on BIORUTA. From this vantage point, Kelvin and Harper could see the interconnectedness of the various regions they had explored.

At the Peaks of Solitude, they set up an observation camp, using Harper's equipment to study the star alignments and their relation to the locations they had discovered. The patterns they observed further confirmed their theory of a sophisticated ancient civilization that had mastered the art of interplanetary connection.

Descending from the peaks, Kelvin and Harper ventured into the Depths of Silence, a vast desert that stretched beyond the horizon. The desert was a place of introspection, where the silence was so profound it seemed to echo. Here, they contemplated the journey they had undertaken, the discoveries they had made, and the friendship they had forged.

In the midst of the desert, they discovered an underground cavern system with walls covered in murals and inscriptions. These inscriptions told the story of a great event, a celestial convergence that had opened a pathway between BIORUTA and Mars. This event, they realized, might be the key to understanding the disappearance of Kelvin's family and the ancient connection between their worlds.

As they left the Depths of Silence, Kelvin and Harper knew they were on the cusp of unraveling a mystery that spanned centuries and galaxies. Their journey together had become more than a quest for answers; it was a journey of discovery about the past and a journey of hope for the future.

In the vast and wondrous world of BIORUTA, their adventure continued, a journey of exploration, discovery, and the unbreakable bonds of friendship. Kelvin and Harper's story was a testament to the power of unity, the pursuit of knowledge, and the enduring quest for understanding in the magnificent tapestry of life.

Kelvin and Harper, with a renewed sense of purpose, set out towards the Twilight Fjords, a region where the sea carved deep into the land, creating a series of dramatic inlets surrounded by steep cliffs. The fjords were known for their mystical atmosphere, where the light of day and night seemed to merge, casting a perpetual twilight over the waters.

As they navigated the fjords, Kelvin and Harper's bond strengthened, their skills complementing each other's perfectly. Kelvin's keen instincts and deep connection to nature, combined with Harper's technological prowess and strategic thinking, made them an effective team. The fjords presented them with new challenges, from navigating the complex waterways to understanding the unique ecosystem of the region.

In one of the fjords, they discovered an ancient underwater ruin, visible only during low tide. The ruin bore striking similarities to the structures they had found in other parts of BIORUTA, further suggesting a planet-wide civilization that had a profound understanding of and connection to the cosmos.

Their exploration of the Twilight Fjords led them to a secluded cove, where they encountered a group of elders who practiced an ancient form of star-based navigation. These elders shared their knowledge with Kelvin and Harper, revealing that the positions of the stars and planets played a crucial role in the ancient travel routes between BIORUTA and Mars.

With new knowledge in hand, Kelvin and Harper ventured towards the Glistening Meadows, a region where the night sky reflected off the dew-covered fields, creating a mirror image of the stars on the ground. Here, they hoped to find a celestial alignment that matched the pattern they had discovered in their research.

The Glistening Meadows were a place of beauty and serenity. At night, the meadows transformed into a living star map, with each dewdrop reflecting the light of a star. It was here that Harper made a crucial observation – the reflection of a specific star alignment on the meadows matched the alignment they had seen in the ancient observatory and the star maps.

Excited by this discovery, Kelvin and Harper realized they were close to unlocking the secrets of the ancient pathways between their worlds. They hypothesized that certain locations on BIORUTA acted as natural conduits for interplanetary travel, aligned with specific celestial events.

Their journey then took them to the Radiant Valleys, a series of valleys where bioluminescent plants and creatures created a landscape aglow with natural light. The valleys were a testament to the wonder of BIORUTA, a planet where the natural world was imbued with a sense of magic and mystery.

In the Radiant Valleys, Kelvin and Harper encountered a variety of luminous creatures, each adding to the enchantment of the region. As they delved deeper into the valleys, they discovered a series of ancient markers that formed a path leading to a hidden temple, shrouded in bioluminescent light.

The temple, once inside, revealed a network of star charts and celestial models, aligning with the findings from their previous explorations. It was clear that the temple had been a center of astronomical study and interplanetary communication.

Their findings in the Radiant Valleys were a significant piece of the puzzle. Kelvin and Harper now had a clearer picture of the ancient civilization's knowledge of the stars and their ability to traverse the space between BIORUTA and Mars.

As they left the Radiant Valleys, Kelvin and Harper knew that their next destination would bring them even closer to unraveling the ancient mysteries. Their journey had become more than a mission; it was a testament to the enduring spirit of discovery and the bonds formed through shared purpose and adventure.

In the vast and wondrous world of BIORUTA, Kelvin and Harper's journey of exploration, discovery, and friendship continued, a journey that transcended worlds and time, bound by the quest for understanding and the unbreakable bonds of companionship.

As Kelvin and Harper departed from the Radiant Valleys, their journey as allies had forged a deep and unbreakable bond. Together, they had traversed the diverse landscapes of BIORUTA, uncovering secrets that spanned time and space. Each discovery had brought them closer not only to unraveling the mysteries of their planets but also to understanding each other's worlds and cultures. With every step, they grew more determined to unveil the truth behind the ancient connection between BIORUTA and Mars and the role of Kelvin's family in this cosmic narrative. As the second chapter of their journey closed, they stood together, ready to face whatever mysteries lay ahead, united by a shared mission and a friendship that transcended their differences.

CHAPTER 3: SECRETS OF THE ANCIENTS

Kelvin and Harper's travels led them to a remote part of BIORUTA, where ancient ruins whispered of a time long forgotten. Amidst these ruins, they discovered the entrance to an underground temple, hidden from the world for centuries. The temple was a labyrinth of corridors and chambers, adorned with intricate carvings and murals depicting the stars and celestial events.

Deep within the temple, Kelvin and Harper found a hidden library, its shelves laden with scrolls and tomes of ancient knowledge. The air was thick with the scent of aged parchment and forgotten tales. Among these texts, they discovered writings that spoke of a grand celestial event, a convergence of planets and stars that had the power to bridge worlds.

The library revealed that Kelvin's family had been guardians of this knowledge, playing a crucial role in the celestial event. They were part of a lineage that had passed down the secrets of the stars from generation to generation, protectors of a cosmic legacy that connected BIORUTA and Mars.

Armed with this new knowledge, Kelvin and Harper realized the significance of their journey. It was not just a quest to reunite Kelvin with his family but a mission to fulfill an ancient legacy and maintain the cosmic balance between their worlds.

CHAPTER 4: THE CELESTIAL ALIGNMENT

With the celestial event drawing near, Kelvin and Harper journeyed to the Pillars of Harmony, a sacred site where the guardians of BIORUTA's ancient knowledge gathered. The pillars were colossal structures, standing tall against the sky, resonating with the energy of the impending alignment.

At the Pillars of Harmony, Kelvin and Harper joined forces with the guardians, a diverse group of beings dedicated to preserving the balance of the cosmos. Together, they prepared for the celestial event, performing rituals and aligning the pillars to channel the cosmic energies.

As the alignment approached, challenges arose. Natural phenomena began to occur across BIORUTA, from unusual weather patterns to shifts in the planet's magnetic fields. Kelvin and Harper worked tirelessly with the guardians, using their combined knowledge and skills to stabilize these anomalies and maintain the balance.

During their preparations, Kelvin and Harper faced trials that tested their courage and resolve. They encountered beings resistant to their efforts, skeptical of the ancient prophecies and fearful of the changes the alignment might bring. Through diplomacy and understanding, they worked to unite all factions, emphasizing the importance of the event for both BIORUTA and Mars.

As the day of the celestial alignment arrived, Kelvin, Harper, and the guardians stood together at the Pillars of Harmony. They watched as the planets and stars aligned, creating a breathtaking tapestry in the sky. The pillars hummed with energy, a cosmic symphony that resonated through the land.

In that moment, Kelvin and Harper realized the significance of their journey. It was a culmination of a legacy that spanned galaxies, a moment of unity and balance that bridged worlds. The celestial alignment was not just an astronomical event but a symbol of the interconnectedness of all life, a testament to the enduring bonds formed in the pursuit of a greater understanding.

As the alignment reached its peak, the air shimmered with energy, and a pathway opened, revealing truths about Kelvin's family and the ancient connection between their worlds. In the vast and wondrous world of BIORUTA, their journey of discovery and unity continued, a journey that transcended time and space, bound by the quest for knowledge and the unbreakable bonds of friendship.

As the celestial alignment reached its zenith, the Pillars of Harmony glowed with an ethereal light, casting an otherworldly radiance over everyone gathered. Kelvin and Harper, alongside the guardians, watched in awe as the sky danced with colors previously unseen, a cosmic ballet that symbolized the union of their two worlds.

In this transcendent moment, a gateway materialized between the pillars, pulsating with energy. The guardians whispered that this was the Pathway of Stars, a bridge created by the celestial alignment that connected distant worlds. Kelvin's heart raced with anticipation; this might be the key to finding his family and unraveling the full extent of their legacy.

As they stepped closer to the gateway, Kelvin and Harper could feel a gentle pull, an invitation from the cosmos itself. With a nod from the guardians, they stepped through the portal, embarking on a journey beyond the confines of BIORUTA.

They emerged on a Martian landscape, one that Harper recognized but was vastly different from the Mars she knew. It was a Mars from another time, vibrant and alive, a stark contrast to the red, barren planet of her era. They realized they had not only traversed space but time as well.

In this ancient version of Mars, Kelvin and Harper discovered a society that thrived in harmony with its environment. The Martians they met were advanced in both technology and spirituality, living in a way that balanced progress with the preservation of their world. Harper was amazed to see her home planet in such a state, flourishing with life and energy.

Their journey on Mars led them to an ancient archive, where they uncovered the history of the interplanetary connection. Kelvin's family, it turned out, were part of an ancient order that had safeguarded the knowledge of celestial pathways, working closely with Martian counterparts to maintain the cosmic balance.

As they delved deeper into the archives, Kelvin and Harper learned about an impending cosmic threat that had led to the sealing of the pathways, a necessary act to protect both BIORUTA and Mars. Kelvin's family had played a crucial role in this, sacrificing their ability to

return to their home in order to seal the pathway and preserve the balance of the cosmos. The weight of this revelation hit Kelvin with a mix of pride and sadness. His family had been heroes, guardians who had acted selflessly for the greater good.

While exploring the Martian archives, Harper discovered technological blueprints and astral calculations that provided insights into the ancient society's advancements in interstellar travel and cosmic energy harnessing. This knowledge was not only a testament to the Martian civilization's achievements but also held potential solutions to the environmental challenges facing Mars in Harper's time.

Kelvin and Harper realized that their journey was not just about uncovering the past; it was also about shaping the future. The knowledge they were gathering had the power to change the fate of both BIORUTA and Mars, potentially reopening pathways and fostering a new era of interplanetary cooperation and harmony.

Their time on Mars was limited, as the celestial alignment that had opened the Pathway of Stars was nearing its end. Before returning to BIORUTA, Kelvin had a heartfelt encounter with the spirits of his ancestors, who expressed their pride in his bravery and determination. They entrusted him with the continuation of their legacy, to be a guardian of the cosmic balance and a bridge between worlds.

With heavy hearts but a renewed sense of purpose, Kelvin and Harper stepped back through the gateway, returning to the Pillars of Harmony on BIORUTA. The guardians greeted them with reverence, recognizing the significance of their journey and the knowledge they had brought back.

In the aftermath of the celestial alignment, Kelvin and Harper worked with the guardians to disseminate the knowledge they had gained. They shared the history of the ancient connection between BIORUTA and Mars, the importance of maintaining the cosmic balance, and the potential for future cooperation between their planets.

The Pillars of Harmony, once a site of ancient rituals, became a beacon of hope and unity. Kelvin and Harper's journey had ignited a spark of curiosity and wonder across BIORUTA, inspiring others to look to the stars with a new understanding of their place in the cosmos.

Kelvin and Harper stood together at the Pillars, looking up at the stars that had guided their journey. They had faced challenges and uncovered mysteries that had changed them forever. Their journey was a testament to the power of friendship, the quest for knowledge, and the unbreakable bonds that form when individuals unite for a cause greater than themselves.

In the vast and wondrous world of BIORUTA, their adventure had become a symbol of hope and unity, a story that would be told for generations to come, inspiring others to explore the mysteries of the cosmos and the bonds that connect all beings.

As Kelvin and Harper continued their work with the guardians at the Pillars of Harmony, they began to understand the broader implications of their discoveries. The knowledge they had brought back from Mars wasn't just historical; it had practical applications that could benefit both BIORUTA and Mars in the present.

They collaborated with the guardians to develop a plan for sharing this knowledge. The first step was to establish a council that included representatives from various regions of BIORUTA and delegates from Mars. This council would oversee the integration of the ancient knowledge into current practices, ensuring that the balance between the two planets was maintained.

One of the key initiatives was the restoration of certain ancient sites on BIORUTA that were aligned with celestial energies. Kelvin and Harper, along with a team of experts, traveled to these sites, using the Martian blueprints to reactivate them. These sites began to function as centers for learning and research, attracting scholars, scientists, and explorers from across BIORUTA and even Mars.

During their travels, Kelvin and Harper also worked on addressing the environmental challenges that both planets faced. They utilized the advanced Martian technology, combined with BIORUTA's natural resources, to develop sustainable solutions. This included new methods of energy production, water conservation, and ecosystem restoration.

As they embarked on these projects, Kelvin and Harper faced challenges. There were those who doubted the wisdom of reopening connections between the planets, fearing the unknown or potential threats. Kelvin and Harper, along with the council, worked tirelessly to address these concerns, promoting understanding and cooperation through transparency and dialogue.

Their efforts began to bear fruit. The celestial alignment had not only opened a pathway between worlds but had also sparked a renaissance of sorts. BIORUTA and Mars started exchanging ideas, resources, and even ambassadors, fostering a new era of interplanetary relations.

In the midst of this progress, Kelvin never lost sight of his personal journey. He found a sense of closure and purpose in continuing his family's legacy. Harper, too, found a new calling in this endeavor, seeing a future where Mars could learn from BIORUTA's connection to nature and its harmonious way of life.

Kelvin and Harper stood at one of the reactivated ancient sites, now a bustling hub of activity and collaboration between BIORUTA and Mars. They looked up at the stars, reflecting on their journey. It had been a path of discovery, challenge, and growth, bringing them closer not only to each other but also to their respective worlds.

Their story had become a beacon of hope, showing that even in the vastness of the cosmos, connections could be formed, differences could be bridged, and a shared future could be forged. The journey of Kelvin and Harper, two unlikely allies brought together by fate, had evolved into a symbol of unity and the endless possibilities that lay in the stars.

As the final days of their work at the reactivated sites came to a close, Kelvin and Harper stood atop the ancient Pillars of Harmony, now a symbol of interstellar unity and cooperation. They had faced numerous challenges, navigated complexities both earthly and cosmic, and had emerged as pioneers of a new era. The celestial alignment had not only bridged worlds but had also ignited a flame of curiosity and collaboration that would continue to burn bright. Kelvin, carrying the legacy of his ancestors, and Harper, a bridge between her Martian heritage and her experiences on BIORUTA, looked out across the horizon, ready for the next chapter of their incredible journey.

CHAPTER 5: NEW HORIZONS

In the aftermath of the celestial alignment, BIORUTA underwent a transformation. Regions of the planet, influenced by the reactivated ancient sites and the influx of Martian technology, began to reveal new secrets and phenomena. Kelvin and Harper, driven by their insatiable curiosity and sense of responsibility, embarked on a journey to explore these transformed regions and deepen their understanding of the planet and its cosmic connections.

Their first destination was the Sea of Serenity, a vast ocean that had begun to exhibit unusual tidal patterns and bioluminescent phenomena. Here, they discovered new marine species and underwater formations that were previously unknown. Harper's technological expertise and Kelvin's intuitive connection with nature allowed them to study these phenomena, revealing insights into BIORUTA's aquatic ecosystems and their response to cosmic influences.

As they journeyed from one region to another, Kelvin and Harper observed profound changes. In the Whispering Forest, the trees now hummed with a more palpable energy, their whispers echoing ancient Martian chants. In the Echoing Cliffs, new acoustic properties emerged, creating harmonies that resonated with the frequencies of Mars.

Their travels took them to the Crystal Desert, where the sands had begun to form patterns that mirrored constellations, a celestial map etched upon the earth. Here, they unearthed artifacts that hinted at ancient interplanetary travel, suggesting that the desert had once been a gateway to other worlds.

Throughout their journey, Kelvin and Harper continued to learn about their roles in the larger narrative. They were not merely observers or participants in this cosmic story; they were catalysts for change and understanding. Kelvin, with his deep connection to BIORUTA and its history, found himself more in tune with the planet's rhythms and secrets. Harper, with her knowledge of Martian technology and her experiences on BIORUTA, bridged the gap between the ancient and the modern, the earthly and the cosmic.

Their exploration led them to the Valley of Echoes, a place where the fabric of space and time seemed thinner, more malleable. Here, they experienced visions of BIORUTA's past and potential futures, glimpses of parallel realities where different choices had led to different outcomes. These visions deepened their understanding of the fluid nature of time and the interconnectedness of all possible timelines.

As Kelvin and Harper progressed across BIORUTA became more than a mission of exploration; it was a journey of self-discovery and realization. They understood that their roles in the larger narrative were not predetermined but were shaped by their actions and choices.

Their journey across the transformed BIORUTA culminated in a return to the Pillars of Harmony, where their adventure had taken a significant turn. Standing once again atop the ancient structure, they reflected on their experiences, the knowledge gained, and the friendships formed. The journey had changed them, and in turn, they had changed BIORUTA and the understanding of its place in the cosmos.

Looking out into the starlit sky, Kelvin and Harper knew that their journey was far from over. The alignment had opened new horizons, not just for them but for all of BIORUTA and Mars. With a sense of wonder and anticipation for the future, they prepared to embark on the next chapter of their adventure, ready to face new challenges and uncover further mysteries in the vast and wondrous universe.

In the continuing journey of Chapter 5, Kelvin and Harper ventured beyond the familiar territories of BIORUTA to regions that were transformed in the wake of the celestial alignment. One such area was the Luminous Plains, where the grasses and wildflowers had begun to emit a soft, radiant glow at night, creating a landscape that resembled a starlit sky.

As they traversed the Luminous Plains, Kelvin and Harper conducted studies to understand the changes. They discovered that the flora had adapted to absorb and store cosmic energy, a phenomenon that was previously unheard of on BIORUTA. This discovery hinted at a deeper connection between the planet and the cosmos, one that was only just beginning to be understood.

Their journey then took them to the Cascading Peaks, where the mountain streams now flowed with water that sparkled with a crystalline quality. Here, they found that the water had unique properties, promoting growth and vitality in the surrounding ecosystem. Kelvin theorized that the water was being charged with cosmic energy, a theory that Harper's tests confirmed.

In the Shadowed Canyons, a region known for its deep chasms and crevices, Kelvin and Harper observed new geological formations. The canyons seemed to be expanding, revealing new layers of rock and mineral that resonated with energy from the celestial alignment. This led to a groundbreaking discovery of minerals with properties similar to those found on Mars, further strengthening the connection between the two worlds.

As they continued their explorations, Kelvin and Harper came to understand that their roles in the larger narrative were not just as observers or catalysts but as stewards and protectors. They saw how the celestial alignment had brought changes that, while beautiful and awe-inspiring, also required care and understanding to maintain the balance of BIORUTA's ecosystems.

One of their most profound experiences occurred in the Mystic Glaciers, where the ice had begun to emit a soft luminescence, casting an ethereal light across the frozen landscape. Within these glaciers, they discovered ancient microbial life that had been dormant for millennia, now awakening due to the changes brought by the alignment. This discovery opened up new possibilities for understanding the origins and resilience of life on BIORUTA.

Kelvin and Harper's journey across the transformed regions of BIORUTA was not only a journey of scientific discovery but also a journey of personal growth. They learned to see the world through each other's eyes, appreciating the beauty and complexity of BIORUTA in new ways. Their friendship deepened, forged in the fires of shared experiences and mutual respect for each other's knowledge and abilities.

Kelvin and Harper found themselves back at the Pillars of Harmony, where their journey had taken a pivotal turn. Standing amidst the ancient stones, they looked out at the horizon, where the sky met the land in a promise of endless possibilities.

The journey they had embarked on had changed them and the world around them. They had uncovered secrets of the ancients, bridged the gap between two planets, and witnessed the transformative power of the cosmos. As they prepared for the next chapter of their adventure, they knew that the horizon held new mysteries to explore, new challenges to face, and new horizons to discover in the magnificent tapestry of life.

In the latter part of Chapter 5, Kelvin and Harper ventured towards the Singing Dunes, a vast desert where the sands were said to produce melodic tones when the winds swept over them. Post-alignment, the dunes had begun to resonate with deeper, more harmonious tones, creating a symphony that echoed the cosmic energies.

Exploring the Singing Dunes, they found that the sands had formed unique patterns resembling star constellations. These patterns seemed to change with the movement of the celestial bodies, suggesting a dynamic connection between the dunes and the cosmos. Kelvin and Harper collected samples and made recordings, hoping to decipher the deeper meaning behind these celestial harmonies.

Their journey then led them to the Shimmering Lakes, a series of interconnected lakes whose waters had taken on a pearlescent sheen since the alignment. The lakes' transformation had a profound effect on the local ecosystem, promoting an explosion of life and diversity. Kelvin and Harper conducted ecological surveys, documenting the changes and ensuring that the balance of the ecosystem was maintained.

In each of these transformed regions, Kelvin and Harper conducted workshops and seminars with local inhabitants and visiting scholars from both BIORUTA and Mars. They shared their findings, fostering a collaborative atmosphere where knowledge was exchanged, and new ideas were born. This collaborative approach led to a deeper understanding of the changes and how best to adapt to them.

As they neared the end of their journey across the transformed regions of BIORUTA, Kelvin and Harper arrived at the Obsidian Cliffs, towering structures of volcanic rock that had begun to emit a soft glow, pulsating in rhythm with the planetary alignment. Here, they discovered ancient inscriptions that had been revealed by the glow, offering new insights into the historical connection between BIORUTA and Mars.

The inscriptions spoke of a time when the two planets had worked in harmony, sharing knowledge and resources for the betterment of both worlds. This historical perspective provided Kelvin and Harper with a blueprint for how BIORUTA and Mars could interact in the present, fostering a relationship based on mutual respect and cooperation.

As they stood atop the Obsidian Cliffs, looking out over the transformed landscapes of BIORUTA, Kelvin and Harper reflected on their journey. They had started as individuals from different worlds, brought together by circumstance. Now, they stood as partners, united in their quest to understand and protect the delicate balance of the cosmos.

Kelvin and Harper returning to the Pillars of Harmony, where their journey had taken on a new dimension. They had come full circle, but they were no longer the same individuals who had started this journey. They had grown, learned, and forged a bond that was as enduring as the stars themselves.

Their journey had shown them the beauty and complexity of the cosmos, the interconnectedness of all life, and the importance of stewardship and cooperation. As they prepared for the next chapter of their adventure, Kelvin and Harper knew that the horizon held endless possibilities, new discoveries, and further opportunities to deepen their understanding of BIORUTA, Mars, and the vast universe they inhabited.

Kelvin and Harper, inspired by their experiences at the Obsidian Cliffs, set out to explore more of BIORUTA's transformed regions. Their next destination was the Aurora Meadows, a once-ordinary grassland that had begun to exhibit extraordinary nocturnal light displays, akin to the northern lights of Earth.

As they camped in the Aurora Meadows under the mesmerizing light show, Kelvin and Harper discussed the potential causes of these phenomena. Harper hypothesized that the celestial alignment might have altered the planet's magnetic field, affecting the atmosphere in ways that were both beautiful and scientifically significant. Kelvin, with his deep connection to BIORUTA, sensed a harmonization of energies, a planet singing in tune with the universe.

Their exploration of the Aurora Meadows led to a chance encounter with a group of BIORUTAn scientists who were studying the same phenomena. Together, they set up an array of instruments to measure the atmospheric changes. The data collected provided valuable insights into the long-term ecological impacts of the celestial alignment and helped predict future atmospheric conditions.

Continuing their travels, Kelvin and Harper ventured to the Sapphire Caverns, an extensive network of underground caves known for their striking blue crystal formations. Since the alignment, the crystals had started to pulsate with an inner light, creating a breathtaking underground landscape.

In the depths of the Sapphire Caverns, Kelvin and Harper discovered ancient murals depicting celestial events. These murals, illuminated by the glowing crystals, detailed a historical account of previous alignments and their effects on BIORUTA. The murals also hinted at a deep-rooted connection between the planet's core and the cosmic events, a connection that was only beginning to be understood in the wake of the recent alignment.

As they journeyed from the Sapphire Caverns, Kelvin and Harper realized that their roles in this larger narrative were evolving. They were no longer just witnesses to BIORUTA's transformations; they were becoming active participants in shaping the planet's response to these cosmic changes. They started to conduct workshops and discussions with local communities, sharing their knowledge and empowering the inhabitants of BIORUTA to become stewards of their changing world.

One of their most significant stops was at the Echoing Valley, a vast expanse where the wind created haunting melodies as it passed over the uniquely shaped rock formations. Here, they found that the valley's natural acoustics had been enhanced since the alignment, creating sounds that were almost musical in nature.

Kelvin and Harper collaborated with sound experts and musicians from across BIORUTA to record and study these melodies. They discovered that the frequencies of the sounds were in harmony with the vibrations detected in the Sapphire Caverns and Aurora Meadows, suggesting a planetary symphony that was responding to the celestial alignment.

As they continued to traverse the transformed regions of BIORUTA, Kelvin and Harper's understanding of the planet deepened. They were witnessing a world reborn, adapting and evolving in response to cosmic forces. Their journey was a tapestry of discovery, each experience weaving into the next, forming a picture larger and more intricate than they had ever imagined.

Their exploration in brought them to a profound realization: the changes occurring on BIORUTA were not isolated events but parts of a grand, interconnected cosmic dance. In the vast and wondrous world of BIORUTA, their journey continued, an odyssey of exploration and understanding, driven by the unquenchable desire to unravel the mysteries of the cosmos and their place within it.

As Kelvin and Harper concluded their journey through the transformed regions of BIORUTA, they found themselves atop the Serene Vista, a high plateau offering a panoramic view of the planet's diverse landscapes. Standing there, they reflected on their journey through the Aurora Meadows, the Sapphire Caverns, and the Echoing Valley, among other marvels. The experiences had not only deepened their understanding of BIORUTA but had also shown them the resilience and adaptability of life in the face of cosmic changes.

The journey had transformed them in profound ways. Kelvin, with his deep connection to BIORUTA, had grown more in tune with the planet's rhythms and secrets. Harper, through her experiences, had developed a new perspective on the importance of harmonizing technological advancement with the natural world. Together, they had become ambassadors of a new paradigm, one that embraced the interconnectedness of all things.

Their final task was to compile their findings and experiences into a comprehensive report. They presented their research to the council, consisting of representatives from BIORUTA and Mars, and shared their stories with communities across the planet. Their work sparked a global conversation about the future, emphasizing the need for balance and cooperation between technology, nature, and the cosmos.

Kelvin and Harper's journey through the New Horizons of BIORUTA culminated in a grand assembly at the Pillars of Harmony, where beings from across the planet gathered to hear their findings. They spoke of the beauty and mysteries they had witnessed, the importance of stewardship for the planet, and the potential for a future that embraced both the wonders of the cosmos and the sanctity of the natural world.

As they concluded their presentation, the assembly erupted in applause, a recognition of their incredible journey and the new era it heralded. Kelvin and Harper stood together, humbled and gratified, knowing that their journey had ignited a spark of hope and curiosity that would burn for generations to come.

As the sun set on the Serene Vista, casting a warm glow over the assembled crowd, Kelvin and Harper looked out over BIORUTA, their hearts full of gratitude for the journey and anticipation for the future. Their story, a testament to the power of friendship and discovery, was just one chapter in the ongoing saga of BIORUTA and its place in the cosmos. The journey ahead was vast and uncharted, but they were ready to face it together, guided by the stars and the unbreakable bonds they had formed.

In the vast and wondrous world of BIORUTA, their adventure continued, a journey of exploration, unity, and the enduring quest for understanding in the magnificent tapestry of life.

EPILOGUE: PATHS DIVERGE

Under the soft glow of the twilight sky, Kelvin and Harper stood at the edge of the Pillars of Harmony, the site that had been the epicenter of their incredible journey. The air was filled with a sense of tranquility, a fitting atmosphere for their farewell. They looked at each other, companions who had traversed the breadth of BIORUTA, faced challenges, and uncovered mysteries that bridged worlds.

Kelvin, the Golden Retriever with a spirit of adventure and a heart bound to BIORUTA, felt a deep gratitude towards Harper. She had not only been a partner in their quest but had also become a dear friend, someone who had helped him understand the vastness of the cosmos and the importance of his role in it.

Harper, the Martian trooper who had arrived on BIORUTA as part of an interplanetary exchange, had found more than she had ever hoped for. In Kelvin, she had found a friend who showed her the beauty and mysteries of a world so different from her own. Their journey together had changed her, giving her new insights and a renewed purpose for when she returned to Mars.

As they prepared to part ways, Kelvin and Harper shared a moment of reflection. They spoke of the landscapes they had explored, the secrets they had unveiled, and the changes they had witnessed. They talked about the ancient connections between BIORUTA and Mars, the celestial alignment, and the transformative effects it had on both planets.

Kelvin expressed his intention to continue exploring BIORUTA, to be a guardian of its mysteries, and to share the knowledge they had gathered. He felt a deep responsibility to his home planet, a desire to protect and understand it more each day.

Harper shared her plans to return to Mars, armed with new knowledge and experiences that could benefit her world. She spoke of implementing the sustainable practices they had discovered and fostering a deeper connection between Mars and BIORUTA. Her time on BIORUTA had given her a unique perspective that she was eager to share with her people.

As they said their goodbyes, there was a promise of keeping the bonds they had formed alive. They agreed to continue sharing their findings and to work towards strengthening the relationship between their planets. Their farewell was not an end but a new beginning, a divergence of paths that would continue to be connected by the stars.

Kelvin watched as Harper boarded her spacecraft, bound for Mars. As the ship ascended into the sky, he felt a mix of sadness and pride. Their journey together might have ended, but the adventure continued, with each of them playing a crucial role in their respective worlds.

Standing alone, Kelvin looked up at the stars, thinking of Harper and the journey they had shared. He turned and gazed out over BIORUTA, his heart filled with excitement for the path ahead. The adventure had changed him, and he was eager to continue exploring, learning, and protecting the beautiful planet he called home.

In the vast and wondrous world of BIORUTA, Kelvin's adventure continued, a testament to the enduring spirit of exploration and the bonds that form in the quest for knowledge and understanding.

His story, interwoven with Harper's, would remain a symbol of the unity and cooperation that had blossomed between their worlds, a beacon of hope in the magnificent tapestry of the cosmos.

ABOUT THE AUTHOR

CARSON J KELLY

Greetings, I am Carson Kelly, a self-sufficient author and game developer, and I'm delighted to introduce myself as the creator of TALKING DOGS: GLEN'S JOURNEY. My passion for video games, science fiction, and technology has led me on an exhilarating journey into the publishing world.

As a writer, I draw inspiration from a love for science fiction, horror, and children's books, striving to craft unique worlds and characters that ignite the imagination. I am mainly influenced by Kass Morgan's The 100 books, Stephen King's captivating stories like The Shining, and RL Stine's

Goosebumps series.

With TALKING DOGS: KELVIN'S WISH, I endeavor to deliver an extraordinary tale that inspires budding storytellers to create their narratives. My readers will encounter a range of emotions while experiencing the journey of TALKING DOGS: KELVIN'S WISH.

Apart from writing, I am involved in over 75 large and small-scale productions, including novels, comic books, and unique tales from the Talking Dogs universe, which I am developing from my compound. These projects reflect my values and vision to create positive change and reach audiences worldwide.

I hope that TALKING DOGS: KELVIN'S WISH resonates and connects with you. Please visit my official website, www.carsonkellygames.com, to keep up with my upcoming projects, from video games to novels like this one. Let's reach for the stars together as we embark on this journey. Thank you for taking the time to learn about me and my work.

BOOKS BY THIS AUTHOR

STARFALL: CROSSED LOVERS

In a universe where love is forbidden, four individuals find themselves entangled in a web of desire, betrayal, and danger. Vega and Zara, two smugglers on the run from a dangerous organization, find themselves falling for each other amidst their mission. Maya, a powerful political figure, is torn between her duty to her planet and her feelings for Xander, a rogue space explorer with a mysterious past. As they navigate through the treacherous galaxy, their lives become intertwined, leading to unexpected alliances and passionate encounters.

STARFALL: CROSSED LOVERS is a thrilling sci-fi romance that explores the complexities of love in a world filled with danger and adventure. With vivid descriptions of futuristic technology, interstellar travel, and steamy intimacy, this novel will take you on a journey through the stars and leave you wanting more.

STARFALL: MARTIANS RISING

In the thrilling sci-fi novel STARFALL MARTIANS RISING, readers are transported to a vivid and fully-realized universe full of danger and intrigue. The story is set in the year 2179, in a distant future where humanity has colonized the solar system and established a thriving network of space colonies. The red planet Mars has become the center of a fierce power struggle between the ruling government and a rebel faction seeking to overthrow it.

The two main characters, Kit and Lena Nebulon, are both experienced and resourceful space mercenaries at the heart of the story. Together, they must navigate the dangerous terrain of a world on the brink of destruction, battling against powerful forces and dark secrets that threaten to tear them apart. The couple also has two daughters, Ayana and Karsyne, who play a significant role in the story.

Ayana is a bright and talented engineer, following in the footsteps of her mother Lena. Despite being just 18 years old, she is already making significant contributions to the Nebulon family business and is highly respected among her peers. Karsyne, on the other hand, is a skilled fighter, taking after her father Kit. At 21 years old, she is one of the most feared and respected fighters in the galaxy, and her abilities are unmatched.

Throughout the novel, the Nebulon family must navigate a treacherous political landscape filled with powerful factions seeking to gain control of the solar system. They are joined by a diverse cast of characters, each with unique strengths and weaknesses. There's Elara, a brilliant scientist who helps Kit and Lena uncover some of the dark secrets lurking beneath the surface of Mars. Rion is a charming rogue with a heart of gold, and Jax is a tough-as-nails soldier who will stop at nothing to protect his fellow soldiers. Tariq is the brilliant and calculating mastermind behind the rebel faction, and his plans could change the course of history.

The world-building in STARFALL MARTIANS RISING is impressive, and readers will be transported to a fully-realized universe full of intrigue and danger. From the dusty streets of Mars' major cities to the vast, uncharted wilderness beyond, the novel takes readers on a thrilling ride full of unexpected twists and turns.

Overall, STARFALL MARTIANS RISING is a must-read for fans of epic sci-fi adventures. With its well-drawn characters, complex world-building, and heart-pumping action, this novel will keep readers on the edge of their seats from beginning to end. Whether you're a longtime fan of the genre or a newcomer looking for a thrilling read, this novel will surely impress.

STARFALL: INFINITE

STARFALL: INFINITE is a captivating and epic sci-fi novel set in the year 2235, several decades after the catastrophic events of "STARFALL: MARTIANS RISING." The world has been transformed into a desolate wasteland, where remnants of a once-flourishing civilization lay in ruins. In this grim and unforgiving backdrop, Kit, a determined survivor, emerges as a beacon of hope.

As readers embark on this enthralling journey, they witness Kit's relentless pursuit of redemption and justice. Through the eyes of this complex and deeply human character, the novel delves into the profound struggles faced by those navigating a world torn apart by war and devastation. Kit's encounters with other survivors, the discovery of a mysterious new order, and the formation of unlikely alliances paint a vivid portrait of a post-apocalyptic society teetering on the edge of despair.

STARFALL: INFINITE explores themes of resilience, morality, and the indomitable spirit of humanity. It delves into the intricate dynamics of survival, the lengths individuals go to protect themselves and their loved ones, and the power of unity in the face of oppression. Amidst the war-torn landscapes and the morally ambiguous choices, the novel emphasizes the importance of compassion, empathy, and the quest for a better future.

With its rich world-building, compelling characters, and intricate plot, STARFALL: INFINITE immerses readers in a riveting narrative filled with gripping action sequences, unexpected twists, and moments of introspection. It is a poignant reminder that even in the darkest of times, hope can prevail, and the human spirit can rise above unimaginable challenges.

This novel will captivate fans of post-apocalyptic fiction, sci-fi enthusiasts, and anyone who appreciates a thrilling tale that explores the depths of human resilience. STARFALL: INFINITE is not just a story of survival; it is a testament to the power of hope, the strength of unity, and the capacity for redemption in a world on the brink of destruction.

STARFALL: THE TALES OF SAMUEL BLACKBURN

In "STARFALL: THE TALES OF SAMUEL BLACKBURN," you'll embark on an enthralling odyssey through the cosmos with Samuel Blackburn, a space captain whose name resounds through the galaxies. From humble beginnings in the unforgiving Aridus desert, Samuel's heart was set on the stars. His early years were marked by hardship, growing up in a small desert settlement where daily survival was a struggle. Yet, his imagination was fueled by tales of legendary space captains who roamed the galaxies, and his destiny seemed intertwined with the vast cosmic expanse.

This narrative unfolds with stolen holobooks hidden beneath Samuel's threadbare mattress, filled with stories of heroic captains and their grand adventures among the stars. These tales fuel his determination to escape the confines of Aridus and pursue a life among the cosmos.

Samuel's journey takes a daring turn when he stumbles upon a mysterious alien artifact rumored to hold unimaginable power. His quest to uncover the artifact's secrets propels him on a perilous expedition across the galaxy, where he faces both old adversaries and new threats. The intricacies of space politics add layers of complexity to his journey.

Family ties and personal struggles add depth to Samuel's character, making him a compelling hero with whom readers can identify. The book is a thrilling adventure, complete with space battles, intriguing mysteries, and high-stakes revelations that promise to set the stage for the next generation of Blackburns.

"STARFALL: THE TALES OF SAMUEL BLACKBURN" is a captivating sci-fi epic that invites readers to explore the boundless cosmos, where the legacy of the Blackburns and the mysteries of the universe await discovery. It's a story of courage, exploration, and heroism that resonates in the hearts of those who dare to dream among the stars.

STARFALL: THE TALES OF AURORA BLACKBURN

In the sweeping cosmic adventure of "STARFALL: THE TALES OF AURORA BLACKBURN," readers are invited into a universe where political intrigue and action-packed escapades intertwine. Aurora Blackburn, the captivating protagonist, emerges as a beacon of strength and resilience as she grapples with the responsibilities of her heritage.

This captivating space opera takes place in a galaxy teeming with treacherous politics, where power shifts like cosmic tides, and long-buried secrets lie in the depths of the cosmos. As a skilled pilot and adventurer, Aurora not only seeks her place in the universe but endeavors to safeguard her family's legacy while unveiling the mysteries of her father's enigmatic past.

Each chapter unfolds as an enthralling tapestry woven with daring escapades, intricate conspiracies, and alliances formed in the crucible of the unknown. STARFALL presents a universe where the resilience and determination of one woman serve as the guiding star, illuminating the path even in the darkest cosmic nights.

STARFALL: THE TALES OF HARMONY BLACKBURN

In the grand finale of the "STARFALL: THE BLACKBURN TRILOGY," get ready to immerse yourself in a breathtaking world of space, intrigue, and family legacies. "STARFALL: THE TALES OF HARMONY BLACKBURN" introduces readers to Harmony Blackburn, the youngest daughter of the renowned space captain, Samuel Blackburn.

Harmony is not your typical young woman. Possessing a quick wit and a cunning mind, she's thrust into the heart of a perilous conspiracy that threatens to shatter the fragile peace of the galaxy. As dark forces conspire to unleash chaos, Harmony must rise to the occasion, unravel secrets, and confront formidable adversaries, all while preserving the legacy of the Blackburn family.

This epic science fiction adventure takes you on a pulse-pounding journey through uncharted galaxies, where the fate of not just one family but the entire universe hangs in the balance. With unexpected alliances, daring missions, and high-stakes encounters, Harmony Blackburn's quest for truth and justice will keep you on the edge of your seat.

Join Harmony Blackburn in this mesmerizing conclusion to the trilogy as she faces impossible odds, battles against the forces of darkness, and strives to protect all that she holds dear. With intricate plot twists, unforgettable characters, and themes of courage and family, "STARFALL: THE TALES OF HARMONY BLACKBURN" promises an electrifying adventure that will leave you spellbound until the very last page.

STARFALL: HARPERS JOURNEY

"STARFALL: Harper's Journey" is a captivating sci-fi novella that invites readers into a universe brimming with adventure and discovery. At the helm of the Starfarer, a vessel of exploration and hope, is Captain Harper – a bold and intelligent leader, driven by a passion for discovery and a deep sense of duty to the cosmos. Along with her diverse and talented crew, Harper embarks on a journey that takes them to the farthest reaches of the galaxy.

From the mysterious Echoing Expanse to the enigmatic Fringe of Infinity, Harper and her crew navigate through uncharted territories, uncovering ancient artifacts, encountering awe-inspiring phenomena, and making first contact with alien civilizations. Each step of their journey is filled with challenges that test their resolve, from cosmic storms to diplomatic standoffs, revealing the strength and unity of the crew.

As they delve deeper into the unknown, they become ambassadors of the Galactic Nexus Initiative, forging a network of cooperation among the stars. Their journey is not just one of scientific discovery but also of cultural exchange and diplomacy, shaping the future of interstellar relations.

"STARFALL: Harper's Journey" is more than a space adventure; it's a story that captures the essence of human curiosity and the unbreakable bonds of friendship. It's a tale that resonates with hope, unity, and the endless quest for knowledge. Perfect for fans of epic space operas and exploratory science fiction, this novella will leave readers dreaming of the stars and the infinite possibilities they hold.

STARFALL: THE RISE OF SAMUEL

Discover the extraordinary universe of STARFALL with "STARFALL: The Rise Of Samuel," the official prequel to "STARFALL: THE TALES OF SAMUEL BLACKBURN." Unveil the untold backstory of Samuel Blackburn, a character whose destiny intertwines with the cosmos. Dive into a world where heroism is forged in the crucible of adversity, and courage is born in the shadow of darkness. This prequel unravels the enigmatic past that precedes the epic events of "STARFALL: THE TALES OF SAMUEL BLACKBURN," providing you with deeper insights into the legend himself.

Nightmare's Edge

Nightmare's Edge is a thrilling slasher novel that follows a group of teenagers who are forced to confront their deepest fears as they face off against a sadistic killer.

Set in the small town of Millfield, the novel introduces a cast of diverse characters, each with their own unique quirks and motivations. As the story unfolds, tensions rise and alliances are tested as the group struggles to stay alive and uncover the truth behind the killer's motives.

The novel is filled with intense action and heart-stopping horror elements, taking readers on a wild ride of twists and turns as they navigate the dark and dangerous world of Nightmare's Edge.

Written with expert precision and a deep understanding of the slasher genre,

Nightmare's Edge is a must-read for horror fans and anyone who loves a good thrill ride. With its gripping storyline, unforgettable characters, and shocking twists and turns, this novel is sure to keep readers on the edge of their seats until the very last page.

Talking Dogs: Phil's Big Adventure

Get ready for an adventure like no other with "Talking Dogs: Phil's Big Adventure." Join Phil, a lovable talking dog, as he sets out on a journey through a holiday-themed wonderland full of love, happiness, and joy. His destination is a big, beautiful city where he hopes to experience new adventures and make new friends.

Along the way, Phil meets George, a curious turtle, who is also on a mission of his own. The two unlikely companions join forces and set out together, eager to explore the new world around them. They soon discover that the journey is filled with wonder and possibility, and they encounter new challenges and make new friends.

As they navigate the city and its surroundings, Phil and George experience the magic of the world around them, discovering the beauty of nature, the thrill of adventure, and the power of friendship. With each step they take, they learn more about themselves and the world, and their bond grows stronger.

Written and developed by Carson J Kelly, "Talking Dogs: Phil's Big Adventure" is a heartwarming and engaging tale that will take readers on a journey of discovery, friendship, and wonder. This charming story is perfect for children and adults alike, and will inspire readers to embrace the magic of the world around them. Don't miss out on this unforgettable adventure!

Talking Dogs: Glen's Journey

Talking Dogs Glen's Journey is a heartwarming novel that takes readers on an incredible adventure through a magical Christmas village. Written by Carson J Kelly and published by Carson Kelly Publishing, LLC, this captivating tale is perfect for readers of all ages.

The story follows Glen, a brave and determined dog who is on a mission to find other dogs like him to celebrate the Holiday season. Along the way, he meets his loyal and adventurous friend, Hunter, and together they set out to explore the village and discover all of its wonders.

As they journey through the village, they encounter many challenges and obstacles, but with their unwavering determination and spirit of adventure, Glen and Hunter never give up. Throughout their journey, they meet a cast of delightful characters, including other dogs who share their love of adventure and the Holiday season.

What makes Talking Dogs Glen's Journey truly special is the bond that develops between Glen and his friends. They share a sense of camaraderie and loyalty that is both heartwarming and inspiring. Through their trials and tribulations, they learn the true meaning of friendship and the importance of never giving up on your dreams.

As the story draws to a close, readers are left with a sense of wonder and excitement. The possibilities for new adventures are endless, and Glen and his friends are ready for anything. This novel is the perfect gift for anyone who loves animals, adventure, and the magic of the Holiday season.

With its engaging storyline, memorable characters, and beautiful illustrations, Talking Dogs Glen's Journey is a must-read for families everywhere. It is a story that will capture your heart and leave you wanting more, and is sure to become a beloved classic for generations to come.

Talking Dogs: Kelvin's Wish

Talking Dogs: Kelvin's Wish is a captivating science fiction novel set in a futuristic world on the planet BIORUTA. Written by Carson J Kelly and published by Carson Kelly Publishing, LLC, this thrilling adventure follows the story of Kelvin, a Golden Retriever dog who can talk, and his quest to find his missing family.

Kelvin is not your average dog - he possesses extraordinary abilities and high intelligence that allows him to communicate with other animals and humans. Along his journey, he teams up with Harper, a Martian trooper who is on her own mission. Despite their differences, Kelvin and Harper form an unlikely alliance as they journey across the planet, facing numerous obstacles and challenges.

As Kelvin and Harper travel deeper into BIORUTA, they begin to uncover secrets and mysteries that will change the course of their journey forever. They discover that the planet is home to a variety of talking dogs who possess special abilities, as well as high-tech gadgets and advanced technologies that seem straight out of a science fiction film.

With each new discovery, Kelvin and Harper must use their wits and skills to navigate the dangers that lie ahead. From treacherous terrain to hostile enemies, their journey is fraught with peril. But with the help of their newfound companions and their own determination, they press on towards their ultimate goal.

As the story unfolds, readers will be drawn into the captivating world of BIORUTA, with its unique characters and thrilling action sequences. With talking dogs, high-tech gadgets, and heart-pumping adventure, Talking Dogs: Kelvin's Wish is a must-read for fans of science fiction and animal lovers alike.

Talking Dogs: Into The Wilds

Talking Dogs: Into The Wilds is about a good boy named Kelvin and his newly found Martian space friend Harper who is on her own mission.

TALKING DOGS SERIES

Talking Dogs: Phil's Big Adventure

Get ready for an adventure like no other with "Talking Dogs: Phil's Big Adventure." Join Phil, a lovable talking dog, as he sets out on a journey through a holiday-themed wonderland full of love, happiness, and joy. His destination is a big, beautiful city where he hopes to experience new adventures and make new friends.

Along the way, Phil meets George, a curious turtle, who is also on a mission of his own. The two unlikely companions join forces and set out together, eager to explore the new world around them. They soon discover that the journey is filled with wonder and possibility, and they encounter new challenges and make new friends.

As they navigate the city and its surroundings, Phil and George experience the magic of the world around them, discovering the beauty of nature, the thrill of adventure, and the power of friendship. With each step they take, they learn more about themselves and the world, and their bond grows stronger.

Written and developed by Carson J Kelly, "Talking Dogs: Phil's Big Adventure" is a heartwarming and engaging tale that will take readers on a journey of discovery, friendship, and wonder. This charming story is perfect for children and adults alike, and will inspire readers to embrace the magic of the world around them. Don't miss out on this unforgettable adventure!

Talking Dogs: Glen's Journey

Talking Dogs Glen's Journey is a heartwarming novel that takes readers on an incredible adventure through a magical Christmas village. Written by Carson J Kelly and published by Carson Kelly Publishing, LLC, this captivating tale is perfect for readers of all ages.

The story follows Glen, a brave and determined dog who is on a mission to find other dogs like him to celebrate the Holiday season. Along the way, he meets his loyal and adventurous friend, Hunter, and together they set out to explore the village and discover all of its wonders.

As they journey through the village, they encounter many challenges and obstacles, but with their unwavering determination and spirit of adventure, Glen and Hunter never give up. Throughout their journey, they meet a cast of delightful characters, including other dogs who share their love of adventure and the Holiday season.

What makes Talking Dogs Glen's Journey truly special is the bond that develops between Glen and his friends. They share a sense of camaraderie and loyalty that is both heartwarming and inspiring. Through their trials and tribulations, they learn the true meaning of friendship and the importance of never giving up on your dreams.

As the story draws to a close, readers are left with a sense of wonder and excitement. The possibilities for new adventures are endless, and Glen and his friends are ready for anything. This novel is the perfect gift for anyone who loves animals, adventure, and the magic of the Holiday season.

With its engaging storyline, memorable characters, and beautiful illustrations, Talking Dogs Glen's Journey is a must-read for families everywhere. It is a story that will capture your heart and leave you wanting more, and is sure to become a beloved classic for generations to come.

Talking Dogs: Kelvin's Wish

Talking Dogs: Kelvin's Wish is a captivating science fiction novel set in a futuristic world on the planet BIORUTA. Written by Carson J Kelly and published by Carson Kelly Publishing, LLC, this thrilling adventure follows the story of Kelvin, a Golden Retriever dog who can talk, and his quest to find his missing family.

Kelvin is not your average dog - he possesses extraordinary abilities and high intelligence that allows him to communicate with other animals and humans. Along his journey, he teams up with Harper, a Martian trooper who is on her own mission. Despite their differences, Kelvin and Harper form an unlikely alliance as they journey across the planet, facing numerous obstacles and challenges.

As Kelvin and Harper travel deeper into BIORUTA, they begin to uncover secrets and mysteries that will change the course of their journey forever. They discover that the planet is home to a variety of talking dogs who possess special abilities, as well as high-tech gadgets and advanced technologies that seem straight out of a science fiction film.

With each new discovery, Kelvin and Harper must use their wits and skills to navigate the dangers that lie ahead. From treacherous terrain to hostile enemies, their journey is fraught with peril. But with the help of their newfound companions and their own determination, they press on towards their ultimate goal.

As the story unfolds, readers will be drawn into the captivating world of BIORUTA, with its unique characters and thrilling action sequences. With talking dogs, high-tech gadgets, and heart-pumping adventure, Talking Dogs: Kelvin's Wish is a must-read for fans of science fiction and animal lovers alike.

Talking Dogs: Into The Wilds

Talking Dogs: Into The Wilds is about a good boy named Kelvin and his newly found Martian space friend Harper who is on her own mission.

A personal letter to you from Talking Dogs creator Carson Kelly

Thank you for reading Talking Dogs: Kelvin's Wish I hope you enjoyed this story featuring both the awesome and great Kelvin the Golden Retriever and Harper.

I do hope you come back for more awesome stories in the years ahead as there are many to come and hey maybe someday we can check back on Kelvin and Harper and what they have been up to since thier tale in Talking Dogs: Kelvin's Wish.

Well I do not want to keep you here any longer but I do hope you enjoyed this story of Kelvin and Harper and I really really hope this story brought you some joy this holiday season or any season on when you have read this story so thank you very much and we will talk again soon on the next Talking Dogs adventure.